About the Author

M'Lord Chook is a father of three on the wrong side of forty-five that has endured everything his family has thrown at him and come out the other side a stronger man. His interests include martial arts, war-gaming, playing guitar and bass and avoiding his brood like the plague. He is currently in the process of writing a follow up book entitled, "Black Metal Dad: Hunting Unicorns and Other Tales". He lives in Adelaide, Australia, where he begrudgingly shares his house with his wife and children as well as a multitude of animals including reptiles, fish and dogs.

facebook.com/BlackMetalDad

Black Metal Dad
A Journey into the Dark Underbelly of Parenthood

M'Lord Chook

Black Metal Dad
A Journey into the Dark Underbelly of Parenthood

Olympia Publishers
London

www.olympiapublishers.com
OLYMPIA PAPERBACK EDITION

Copyright © M'Lord Chook 2022

The right of M'Lord Chook to be identified as author of
this work has been asserted in accordance with sections 77 and 78
of the Copyright, Designs and Patents Act 1988.

All Rights Reserved

No reproduction, copy or transmission of this publication
may be made without written permission.
No paragraph of this publication may be reproduced,
copied or transmitted save with the written permission of the
publisher, or in accordance with the provisions
of the Copyright Act 1956 (as amended).

Any person who commits any unauthorised act in relation to
this publication may be liable to criminal
prosecution and civil claims for damage.

A CIP catalogue record for this title is
available from the British Library.

ISBN: 978-1-80074-384-7

First Published in 2022

Olympia Publishers
Tallis House
2 Tallis Street
London
EC4Y 0AB

Printed in Great Britain

Acknowledgements

This book is dedicated to my wife, Karen, and my children, Helga, Mugwomp and Boris. Without you in my life, none of the tales told herein would have been possible. The pages that follow may seem to suggest otherwise, but the truth of the matter is, you make me whole. I am a better man because of it.

Thanks a lot. I always wanted to be an evil son of a bitch.

To all of you that I pestered into reading my drafts and providing feedback, helpful or otherwise, I thank you. You tried your best. It's just a shame that your best wasn't very good. Better luck next time.

Last but far from least, a massive, devil-horned salute to my mother, Maleficent, and stepfather, Napoleon. Their support helped bring this project to fruition. My gratitude is eternal.

P.S. A shout out to all the dogs I have known, all those that I know and all those that I have yet to meet. You guys, rock! Keep living your best lives.

Foreword:
Don't Say I Didn't Warn You!

Twenty-five years, give or take.

That's how long it's been since I told myself I was going to write something that people would pay money to read. There were a couple of false starts between then and now but finally here we are. Shit is about to get real.

Before we proceed let me tell you a bit about myself. I'm an oppressed male on the wrong side of forty-five with the mind of a fourteen-year-old boy. I am a second generation Australian whose grandparents on both sides came to Oz from the Ukraine in the aftermath of WW2. My genetic heritage has afflicted me with an ailment called the Eastern European Smile, or E.E.S. More on this shortly. I love my family deeply, but I also love tormenting them to the point where my continued existence isn't assured. In all honesty I have to say the pure joy I get from causing them grief is my reason for living and I have made it a point to become very good at it.

My brain works differently than most. I'm not on the spectrum or anything, I just approach things with a very different mindset. My thought processes are definitely bizarre. Put another way, when it comes to thinking outside the box, I'm so far outside it, the box isn't even visible. This is important to understand from the very beginning as this book isn't your run of the mill rainbows and unicorns parenting guide. This tale most definitely has teeth.

You know those borderline psychotic thoughts that run through your mind when your little parasites won't do what they've been asked for the hundredth time? All while they're emptying the pantry of anything remotely edible and leaving a trail of destruction behind them? You know those thoughts you don't act on because you're a good parent and are too scared of being ass raped in prison for fifteen to twenty years?

This book takes those thoughts and dials them up to eleven. You have been warned.

If there is anything I ask of those brave or foolish enough to give this book a chance, it is: don't take it seriously. Sure, some of the content may cause you to question my sanity, but that's perfectly normal. Many have in the past and I've yet to be committed. My only wish is that what is found within these pages makes you laugh, even just once. Maybe in six months' time when you are remembering a paragraph or two that stood out. While you're a pallbearer at Aunty Irene's funeral perhaps. But that's on you, not me. You should know there is a time and place for laughter and beloved Irene's interment is certainly not it.

Treat this dark glimpse into the existential hell that is parenting as I intended you to. A piece of black comedy taken from the mind of a three-time father and borderline sociopath who regularly misplaces his moral compass.

However, just in case…

As we live in the "Age of the Perpetually Offended" I feel I need to make this clear so Child Protective Services of some stripe don't come kicking down my door. I will touch on some controversial topics and I will make some shocking recommendations when it comes to alternative parenting methods but remember, it is all done with humour at its core. Shocking, Dark, Norwegian Black Metal Burning Churches to Ash humour, but humour nonetheless. Do not, under any circumstances take what is said in this book and apply it to real world parenting. I repeat, if you love your kids like I love mine, DO NOT use this as a guide to raising them. It will end badly for all parties involved.

In fact, if you have intentions of using this as an aid in child rearing, I strongly recommend that you immediately return your copy to the place of purchase and receive a full refund. Failing that, burn it to cinders before you read any further. Then I suggest you contact a reputable mental health professional ASAP. I'm not even kidding.

The Eastern European Smile (E.E.S.): Why I Wrote This Book

As mentioned above I suffer from E.E.S. You from the West have come to call this "Resting Bitch Face". It is a condition where the face of the sufferer is perpetually set in an angry, murderous scowl, even in times he or she may be experiencing great joy. While slowly becoming more common in Western nations, practically every person of Slavic heritage suffers from E.E.S. to some degree.

Now, I have been thrown out of nearly every pub and club I have ever visited. I would estimate seventy percent of those instances are a direct result of Eastern European Smile and not being fall-over drunk. Seventy fucking percent! If I lived in the old country my life would be normal, uneventful even, just like everyone else around me. Here in the supposedly free democracy of Australia, however, I am continuously a victim of prejudice because of an affliction I have no control over. My children's friends will not look me in the eye or even speak to me as they think I want them dead. People in general avoid me as I look angry as fuck all the time. Even after sex.

The history of E.E.S. dates back many hundreds of years. In the nations of Eastern Europe, it was considered a sign of lunacy if one was seen smiling for no apparent reason. So as to avoid being committed to an asylum, people just stopped looking happy. If you could see the photos I have from my family in Ukraine, there is one common feature. No one smiles. Wedding or funeral, the expressions are the same. E.E.S. has become so ingrained into the Slavic psyche it is now part of our genetic makeup. So much so, I live with it even though I have never even been to the old country. While not life-threatening it is life-changing. Sadly, E.E.S.'ers generally have solitary lives due to the fact other people are too frightened to talk to them.

To help society become more educated about this illness, I plan on donating one hundred percent of the proceeds on the sale of this book to the "Understanding E.E.S. Foundation". Their motto, "We all smile on the inside!", inspires me every single motherfucking day.

A Quick Note on Naming Conventions

While digesting this tale of madness, you, the reader, will be exposed to those that call themselves "My Family". For the benefit of all involved their identities have been altered in a manner more pleasing to myself.

The spawn of my loins will henceforth be known by the monikers they would have been given if my significant other of the time just obeyed me like the good wife I signed up for. Needless to say, she wasn't and she didn't, so the children were lumped with much less-inspiring names. Regardless, this is my book and I can do what I want. The eldest daughter will be called Helga, while the middle child, also a girl, shall answer to Mugwomp. Finally, my youngest progeny, the boy child, will be named Boris.

Like many, I have had the misfortune of being married more than once. My first union resulted in the birth of Helga. A relatively bright spark in an otherwise hellish union. I give thanks that something Not Shit came from this stint in the underworld. This beast of a woman will simply be known as Screech.

Bondage to my current source of marital bliss gave rise to my other two "blessings". Without her express permission I will be rebranding my wife with the name Karen because she'll hate it and that makes me smile. You will come to realise that the name is an appropriate one.

Throughout this account other bit players have their parts to play. Their true identities have also been suppressed but due to the truly insignificant roles performed, they will not be listed here. They should count themselves lucky they get a mention at all. While it could be said that providing them with pseudonyms is to protect their identities, in reality it is in case a scenario like this eventuates:

'Hey mate. What's this? I told you I didn't want to be in your book!'

'Nah mate, that's not you. Take it easy,'

'But what about…'

'It's not you man, relax.'

'Hang on, I distinctly remember…'

'Prove it dude.'

Just joking. Everyone represented has given their permission. Honest. Except Screech.

Last but not least, I have also chosen an alias for myself because it amuses me. You'll find that many strange and trivial things, most likely inappropriate, bring me great pleasure. From here on in my tribe will address me simply as "M'Lord". Nice and simple, but most importantly, a title rightly earned. Earned through the hell-spawned trials and tribulations of herding this flock on the journey of life in a less than fatal manner.

Last Chance

So, you have been forewarned. I doubt many of you will have been on a journey quite as random as the one you are about to embark on. Just go with it. Leave all that heavy moral baggage at the door and just enjoy the crazy, metal-as-fuck ride my lucky bunch experience on a daily basis. In fact, I wouldn't be surprised if reading this stimulates the same parts of your brain that get tickled in the head of a young child laughing.

A young child laughing while he cooks live snails on the barbecue.

Who knows, you might even come to enjoy it.

In the words of the great Billy Connolly, "I'm the one going to hell, you were just watching."

Part 1: Pregnancy and V.E.D.

"I am in love with a baby I have not met yet."
   gomamma247.com

"Nine months preparing to fall in love for a lifetime."
   First cry parenting

"I have never read such bullshit in my life!"
   Paul Szewczuk

"AAAAAAAARRRGH!!! I HATE YOU!!!! GET THIS FUCKING THING OUT OF ME!!!!"
   Karen during the delivery of Mugwomp

"Hahahahaha!! This gas is good fucking shit!!"
   M'Lord during the delivery of Mugwomp

Introduction:
Sorry for Bursting Your Bubble

So, it's happened. Either the condom has burst, you were just fucking stupid and engaged in unprotected coitus, or, Satan forbid, you actually planned it. Regardless, you are now expecting a new addition to the tribe. You have my heartfelt condolences.

It's understandable to some extent that first time expectant parents get excited about having a baby. The miracle of life, the unbreakable bond between mother and child, the pride and responsibility of raising a potential leader of humankind; it all sounds so appealing, doesn't it?

The problem is, however, that these beliefs are based on falsehoods. Everything these parenting virgins are told or read is a lie designed to convince them that this family gig is fucking amazeballs. What a crock of shit. The fact that veteran mothers, fathers and even grandparents propagate these untruths is mortifying. Every one of us should be ashamed. We have nothing to gain as a species. The Earth is full. It doesn't need any more oxygen thieves. So why do we insist on convincing others that adding to the gene pool is the right thing to do?

In my not so humble opinion, we do it out of jealousy and spite. Why should some perfectly happy couple, in the prime of their lives, continue to enjoy a childfree existence with all the potential that entails, when we parents give up the best years of our lives rearing ungrateful little shits? Why should they be free to travel the world, enjoying the fine things in life and having bank balances in excess of fifty dollars, while we are forced to endure lives of ceaseless toil filled with unending demands and mountainous debt? It's a case of, "If my life is gonna suck then so should yours!"

Well, no more! I plan on obliterating the lies associated with parenthood. Not only will I invalidate many myths told by guardians the world over, I will back up my claims with real world examples drawn from my extensive experience in the field. These tales may have varying levels of historical accuracy, based on the needs of the story or the quantity of alcohol and narcotics consumed at the time, but the core of the argument remains unchanged: Having kids is a shit-show you shouldn't wish on your worst enemy.

Using the knowledge contained in this manuscript, first time prospective parents will now be able to make an informed choice as to whether they want to continue a life of ease, nothing to concern themselves with other than the gratification of their desires, or to foolishly choose to sacrifice lives full of promise and joy, all so they can create and raise another potential Adolph Hitler or Lizzy Borden.

Likewise, existing parents looking to add to their family will hopefully read this tale of despair and realise that they don't really want any more kids because kids are no damn good. Instead, they decide to adopt a dog. In addition, rather than continuing to propagate the lie that having children is such a rewarding experience, they recommend sterilisation as a viable alternative.

A time of great change is upon us.

I won't be getting bogged down with the changes a woman's body goes through during the incubation period. There are a multitude of texts which examine this stage in exhaustive, needless detail. All that you are required to know is that physically the chest, stomach and posterior regions undergo spectacular growth spurts verging on the mythical. In short, the host begins to look and move like an inflatable boxing clown.

It is in the future Mother's brain that more interesting changes are occurring. Logic and sanity, what little there was, have been replaced with absurdity, mental instability and an unhealthy requirement to have all needs met. Fucking instantly or else! This becomes more prevalent the closer the expectant mother gets to her due date. There is no treatment, and it is just easier for everyone to comply with the huge blow-up clown rather than deal with a rampaging beast from the pits of Hell. Just give them what they want. After all, they're hosting the goddamn Antichrist.

Chapter 1:
Antenatal Classes

A common demand made by these spherical goddesses is the attendance of a series of antenatal classes in preparation for "The Big Day". Notice I said series. For the sole purpose of milking pregnant women of as much money as possible, the charlatans that run these classes spread information that could be divulged in a one hour sitting over a number of sessions.

Around five or six months into Helga's gestation, Screech thought she would approach me to discuss attending some of these classes. The conversation went something like this:

'Hey, M'Lord,' she wheezed.

'Yes Screech?'

'I think we should go to some birthing classes.'

'Why?'

'So we can learn what to do when Helga is due.'

'Why?'

'Because I think it'll be good for us.'

The tone of Screech's voice was noticeably changing. In normal conversation she speaks in a hiss-like manner, much like a serpent. Currently it was approaching the sound a stovetop kettle makes as it boils. Time to stir the pot, I thought to myself.

'Nope.' I stated, deadpan as fuck. E.E.S. can be a boon at times.

Contrary to the advice given previously about giving the pregnant bovines what they want, I had poked the bear and would now suffer the consequences. With a scream that nearly tore the fabric of reality apart, she shrieked:

'I'M BOOKING US IN AND WE ARE BOTH FUCKING GOING ALL RIGHT!'

This was pronounced as one word.

As I wiped her spittle from my face I smirked and replied, 'Gotcha!' while pretending to catch the king of all fish. Screech's skin tone was approaching the colour of molten steel and before she could erupt again, I spoke the words of power.

'Hey, relax babe, of course I'll go. Whatever you want.'

Instantly her anger vanished, but I knew I was standing in the eye of the storm so I followed up with, 'It should be interesting.' Bam! Disaster averted.

I couldn't have been further from the truth. For one and a half hours a week over a ten-week period, I was forced to endure some of the most mind-numbingly tedious tutorials ever experienced by man. I would rather ingest live rats and have them eat their way out of my bowels than attend those classes again.

Our instructor, a nurse we shall call Amelia Dyer (Google her, I dare you), was a humourless individual that spoke in a soul-draining monotone. The bitch should have got a job that she liked.

From memory, there were four or five other couples present, with the expectant mothers all around the same point in their pregnancy. They were freaking huge! It was like being in the middle of a horrific, all-in sumo war. I was surrounded by massive, hormonal boxing clowns and had to tread carefully, lest I be torn to pieces like a leg of lamb thrown to a pack of starving wolves.

I glanced at a few of the other sperm donors and noted our features were all the same: drawn and haggard with dark rings under our eyes. Keeping our Jabba the Hutt wannabes satisfied and docile was taking its toll.

The room the classes were held in appeared to be an abandoned morgue. The neon lighting was so bright our already pale skin appeared corpse-like and our sunken eye-sockets were deep in shadow.

'A fitting place for the likes of us.' I mused to myself.

The expectant mothers were positively radiant though, beaming with an inner glow. This couldn't be anything other than the furnaces of the underworld made manifest in the spawn they harbored in their bellies. They sat around comparing notes and cheerfully pointing out how big each of them were getting while us plebs counted the holes in the asbestos ceiling.

After ten or so minutes of pointless gossip, Dyer motioned us to the mats arranged in a circle on the floor. It should be noted she sat her fat ass in a padded office chair. Yes, that's right, we had to sit on the floor like we were some fucking four-year-old kids getting ready for story time. This was all the more infuriating because there were two stacks of perfectly functional chairs located in the corner. I'm certain this was intentional. Our tutor wanted us to be as uncomfortable as possible so we wouldn't fall asleep. She was successful in her endeavors.

This continued week in, week out, the same prelude to every class. To preserve your sanity, I will not subject you to an in-depth analysis of every hateful lesson attended. What follows is a brief critique of a few of the topics covered.

1) Early Pregnancy

Really? The horse has already bolted on this one. The gravid beasts going to these sessions are all well past "early pregnancy". This information is something that needs to be provided to girls in high school as a form of contraception, not women that have already experienced "The Biggening" first hand.

Zero stars. Do not recommend.

2) Signs and Stages of Labour

To be honest this class was very informative. I hope that I remember everything that I learnt when I too am heavy with child. What a joke.

Sorry but if a woman can't tell when her body is about to spit out a sprog then I seriously doubt she should be having one in the first place. Have you experienced sudden, explosive fluid loss from your nether regions? Are you suffering from periodic abdominal pain that increases in frequency, intensity & duration? It could be gastro, but if you've been pregnant for around nine months then chances are you are going into labour. Have fun.

This class was less informative and more terrifying for the expectant mothers, especially the first timers. You could see the mouths of the poor newbies drop open, Screech included, as they began to realise the enormity of what they will soon experience. Tears began to flow from some of the poor girls' eyes and even veteran birthers started regretting their life choices. Those of us in the room with testicles looked like we had dodged a bullet. I know I wasn't the only one that thanked the Dark Lord for being born a male. Still, to ensure harmony,

I feigned sympathy and comforted Screech by gently patting her on the head.

One star. While still a tedious way to spend an evening, at least this session caused Screech to wish she had been born with male genitalia.

3) Different Birthing Positions

Just like the Satanic Bible has its opposite in the Old and New Testaments, this topic made me realise the Kama Sutra also has its antithesis in this class. Where the Kama Sutra is a manuscript that shows how one can achieve a form of spiritual and sexual enlightenment, this tutorial showed what it would be like if a herd of hippos took up rhythmic gymnastics. There was nothing enlightening about what I witnessed that day.

For the next hour and a half Nurse Dyer put Screech and the rest of the pod through their paces. We alternated between a slide show and having the poor girls mimic what was projected onto a whiteboard. I was amazed at the number of different positions the female of our species had available to them when having a child. And this is just on dry land. When you incorporate water birthing, the choices available are truly mind boggling. For what though? I would have thought lying on your back, legs in the air like a turtle that's been rolled over would be the default position. That or squatting like you're having a shit in the woods.

Not one of the poses that we were shown was going to alleviate any of the horrific pain these women were going to experience during labour, so what was the point in complicating matters? Their befuddled minds were struggling to remember things they had mastered a lifetime ago. How could they be expected to learn anything new? Even if they could, giving them a choice when the time is upon them is a terrible idea. We all know how long it takes for a woman to decide what to wear. By the time they've decided on a birthing position, the poor baby would have already crash landed headfirst onto the hard linoleum floor. No, giving them options at this critical time is a fool's errand. I say, "Keep It Simple, Stupid!"

Except for a couple of positions where I was required to provide support for Screech, my presence at this session was not needed. It wasn't even amusing watching her roll around on a yoga ball like a beached manatee. (These classes were taking their toll on me and I felt myself die a little bit more after each one. I suspected Amelia Dyer was a practitioner of the black arts and was using these lessons to slowly leech my life force. The witch was more of a psychic vampire than my own wife.)

To make it more interesting for us not contorting our bloated bodies, we should have been given scorecards. This would have alleviated our boredom as well as giving the women the impetus to try and outdo one another. We could have even had a bit of a bet on the winner, who would have been awarded a trophy and snacks. Unfortunately, it wasn't to be, so yet again I wasted my precious life appeasing my beastly spouse.

Zero stars. A waste of time and effort for all involved. It could have been one star if only there was a little forethought from our instructor with regards to catering to the needs of everyone present.

4) Relaxing and Breathing Exercises

In theory this session provides tools for the mother-to-be

to utilize during labour. It also instructs her partner how to help the poor woman by counting her breaths, even breathing in time with her as a form of encouragement. Sure, this all works well enough in the classroom, where both parties can bond by breathing and counting in unison without all the mayhem and trauma that comes with actual labour. However, when it's showtime and the pregnant banshee is in the throes of yet another contraction, it is a fool that tries to get their partner to use the exercises taught in this class. Anyone that has participated in a childbirth will attest that this is a surefire way to feel the wrath of the She-Devil; and rightfully so.

Imagine, if you will, the following scenario. You have been on the throne for half an hour trying to squeeze out a shit so huge it threatens to split you in half. You are moaning and grunting as you push and push. Sweat beads on your brow as you struggle with the greatest stool known to man. You feel it slowly inching out of your anus and just when you think you've won, you relax, and WOOSH! it slides straight back up your fucking ass. You have to start all over again.

Now imagine that you have been struggling for four or five hours, not thirty minutes. Also imagine this is not happening in the privacy of your own toilet but in a room with three or four other people, all of whom are taking great interest in your dilemma. A couple of these observers are shit specialists and know how to guide you through this process so you come out the other side a few pounds lighter and relatively unharmed. You trust these two as they are professionals that have helped many others in the same predicament as yourself. You listen to their instructions and follow them to the letter. Then there are the others present. One of them, your partner, sits down next to you and takes your hand. He or she then says to you, 'C'mon babe, breathe with me, you'll be right. I'll help you. One, two, three…

What would your reaction be? If you don't think you would explode at the fucking idiot with righteous fury and leave them cowering in the corner, then you are fooling yourself. I get angry if I'm on the toilet and one of the kids comes to tell me something. Boris could come banging on the door screaming, 'M'Lord! We need your help!'

My response would be something along the lines of, 'For fuck's sake, mate, I'm in the toilet. Go away!'

'But M'Lord, the kitchen is on fire!' he might add.

And I would reply, 'I don't care! I'm having a shit, now piss off!'

And that's just a regular poo. If I was passing a watermelon sized turd and Karen was offering me words of encouragement while huffing like an asthmatic, I would lose my mind. In the same situation I guarantee that you would too.

Well, that's exactly what labour is like. If your partner is in the middle of giving birth to your brat, then all you need to do is sit the fuck down, shut the fuck up and let her squeeze your hand to the point of catastrophic structural failure. She doesn't want you breathing in time with her like you were having some strange as fuck tantric sex session. She doesn't want you imitating The Count from "Sesame Street", especially if you are laughing maniacally between numbers. If she wants you to do anything other than hold her hand or get her a drink, trust me, she'll let you know. Leave the breathing and pushing instructions to the professionals in the room.

Zero stars. This topic needs to be removed from the antenatal curriculum immediately. It provides no practical assistance to the birthing experience at all and following the advice given is potentially life threatening.

5) Breastfeeding

Why did I need to be here? My guess is that it was so Nurse Dyer could consume more of my sweet, irresistible soul, nothing more. After this session was over, I remember thinking that perhaps Screech and Dyer were in cahoots and had some malevolent way of sharing my life force. There could be no other reason for my bitch of a wife making me accompany her to this lesson. I had nothing to gain from being there. I couldn't suckle the newborn Helga when she arrived any more than Screech could wear a cock-ring. I gained no sexual satisfaction from learning about lactation. And there was no way in the nine hells I was going to be required to express milk for future use. Like it or not ladies, this is most definitely women's work.

I'm not even going to rate this piece of shit topic. If your expectant partner insists on attending antenatal classes, even after this review, then I suggest you do everything in your power to avoid this session. Fake your mother's death, anything, but do not go. It's ninety minutes of your life you will never get back.

6) The Birthing Video

Do you remember the joy you felt back in school when you entered a classroom and saw a trolley with a television at the front of the room? You knew it was going to be a nice, easy lesson. No taking notes or spot tests, just watching some bullshit documentary or, if you were lucky, a movie. No doubt it was because your teacher had a bender the night before and didn't want to deal with your shit that day. It didn't matter why though, watching TV in class was always an event to be celebrated. I thought so too, until I went to Nurse Amelia Dyer's final session.

After thanking us for our attendance over these past months and presenting us all with certificates, (Huzzah! I passed Antenatal Class! The world is my oyster. Pffffft, whatever.), she informed us we were going to watch a video of an actual birth. Screech and the rest of the group thought this was a sterling idea. I would have rather watched some porn but it was the last lesson ever so I was in a pleasant frame of mind. Nurse Dyer pressed play on the video recorder, (yes that's how long ago it was), and the footage began. Any preconceived notions of how amazing childbirth was going to be were swiftly crushed like an egg under the heel of a Nazi jackboot. This was like watching a snuff film.

The fear felt by the mummy wannabes when the labour process was explained to us back in session two returned and was magnified ten-fold. Being told what they would go through was a far cry from actually witnessing the process. For the next forty-five minutes we watched a no-holds-barred extravaganza of blood and faecal matter, punctuated with a soundtrack straight from a Cannibal Corpse album. The wails and moans coming from the throat of the woman in the film could not have been produced by human vocal cords. It was as if the lost and the damned had been let loose on the earth. For the finale we were subjected to a midwife's view of a newborn's skull breaching the vagina in an expulsion of gore and embryonic fluid. The mewling little meat puppet was then torn from between the exhausted mother's legs and placed on her breast for the first of its parasitic feedings. With a sadistic grin Amelia stopped the recording and asked the group if there were any questions. She was greeted with a horrified silence.

I looked around the room. Screech's eyes had rolled back in her head like a terrified cow. Other women were visibly choking back tears or vomit. All of them were experiencing a mild case of PTSD. If the goal of antenatal classes was to alleviate some of the fears held by expectant parents, then this final lesson failed abysmally. These women were more petrified than an altar boy in the Vatican. The males in the room all gave each other fist bumps as once more we thanked whatever god we believed in for gifting us penises. Of course, this was done out of sight of our distraught partners. We still valued our lives.

Two stars. This was definitely the highlight of my time with the soul-thief, Amelia Dyer. I got to watch a pretty good independent horror flick. Granted, the special effects were obviously from the 1980's, but the acting was credible and affected the audience in a deeply emotional manner. It also humbled Screech, whose constant declaration of the superiority of the female sex was undone by the simple fact that my genitals ensured I would never feel the excruciating pain of childbirth. That's a win in my books. Finally, this session deserved two stars purely because it provided inspiration for my directorial debut.

Conclusion

I cannot stress how utterly pointless these classes were. They didn't cover anything of use at all. In the end, there are medical professionals present at the delivery that assist with the process at every stage up to its unfortunate conclusion. When my future wife Karen was heavy with Mugwomp she suggested antenatal classes. Before she could finish her sentence, I applied a Vulcan Nerve Pinch to the base of her neck and the issue was never broached again. Avoid them like an anti-vaxxer, dodges needles.

To add insult to injury, Screech ended up having Helga by caesarean section so nothing we were shown was in the least bit relevant. To this day I'm positive this was purely out of spite and didn't have anything to do with the medical advice we were given.

Chapter 2:
Preparing for Baby's Arrival
(AKA: Buy All the Things)

Kids are expensive. So much so you are spending thousands of dollars before they are even born. At least the little fuckers let you get used to burning cash before they come along; because when they do arrive, your money disappears faster than a line of coke from a stripper's ass.

The initial outlay is exacerbated by the fact Future-Mum is using her womb and not her brain to make decisions. And her womb is a greedy son of a bitch. It does not care if a jumpsuit will only be worn for a couple of months before it is outgrown or covered in so many shit stains it is unusable. It does not care if the shoes that are bought for a lump that can't even walk are too small before the child can even take a step. Christ, it doesn't even take into account how quickly the kid is going to grow before it commits to a full wardrobe.

All of these considerations are irrelevant. The Womb wants the best clothes that money can buy. It will also want to paint the nursery in garish, pastel colours "because bubs will love it". Bullshit. Bubs won't even be able to see two feet in front of its nose when it's born. It won't give a fuck what colour its room is. The Womb will want mega cross-country prams, even though it has never gone hiking in its life. This is immaterial because what The Womb wants, The Womb gets.

The Womb should want tiny shock collars, like the ones used on unruly dogs, or tasers, or candy flavored pepper-spray. But no, that will never be the case.

Here is a list of its favourite things and why they are not required.

1) The Cot

We have been brainwashed into believing that this expensive piece of furniture is a necessity. Why? In the times of our grandparents and great-grandparents, infants slept in boxes or dresser drawers without coming to any harm. Only rarely was the child thrown out with the trash or smothered with pantaloons and when it did happen it was more than likely intentional. I can relate to this desire in my ancestors to thin the herd. There have been many times over the years I have wanted to leave Helga, Mugwomp or Boris out for the wolves. Either individually, in pairs, or as a group, depending on who was the cause of my displeasure. In any event I was thwarted by Karen, who has an unhealthy obsession with protecting our spawn.

I would argue that we look further back in time to our primal roots. Have the newborn sleep with dogs. If you don't like dogs, then you are probably subhuman and can't read anyway, so the following points are moot.

It is recommended you get hold of a mating pair of canines and time the pregnancies so both bitches, (human and animal), give birth at the same time. Rather than buying a crib, place your little cocktail of recessive genes amongst the gorgeous pups and mother-dog in a lined box lovingly prepared earlier. The benefits are fourfold.

Firstly, your offspring would be kept warm snuggled

amongst all the cute little balls of love. This will also help develop bonds between your child and the dog pack. Hopefully this results in them being more tolerant of your blob's apparent inability to thrive and incessant need to grab handfuls of their flesh. A reduction in retaliatory attacks by your much more capable fur babies should be guaranteed.

Secondly, when your mini-me grew hungry, it could suckle the teat of its furry wetnurse. Worry not, as this milk is of a much higher nutritional value than the watery fare provided by a human mother. After all, Romulus and Remus would never have founded the Roman Empire if it wasn't for wolf milk.

Thirdly, as you and your partner are well rested due to not having to wake through the night to feed your brat, your home is much more harmonious. This leads to a better family life for all of you. Extensive studies, which may or may not have been undertaken in Siberia, revealed that divorce rates for couples using this method of early child-rearing are fifty times lower than couples raising their child in the traditional manner.

Finally, you have saved a significant amount of money by not having to buy a cot. In actual fact, you have also gained a room due to not needing a nursery.

As a bonus, if your child is born in the warmer months, you can save even more money by not using nappies or clothing. There is no need to worry about your young one soiling itself because as amazing as our four-legged friends are, they have a weakness for baby scat. One of their few flaws, but one that ensures your own hairless pup stays clean without you having to lift a finger.

Some skeptics would argue that the costs involved with caring for a pack of dogs are greater than any savings made in not buying a cot. I tell those naysayers to eat a dick. Any additional expenses incurred in having to raise a litter of pups are more than offset by the proceeds received on their sale. Regardless, there is never any need to justify living with our four-legged friends as they make much better company than our own snot-filled progeny.

My apologies, we will return to the topic at hand. The merits of animal companionship compared to that provided by our own children is covered elsewhere.

As already stated, The Womb wants to have the best of everything for the little beast it harbours inside. When it comes to cots this can get very expensive. Both Karen and Screech wanted to throw down a stack of cash on a piece of furniture that will only get eighteen to twenty-four months use before it was mothballed and superseded by a normal bed. Initially, I argued with both of them in favour of either using a box or the mutually beneficial dog surrogate option. Unsurprisingly, their narrow mindedness ensured that I was flatly refused by each of them in turn. Honestly, it is attitudes like theirs that hold humanity back from reaching its true potential.

A different strategy was required to prevent this gross mismanagement of funds.

What follows has never been disclosed by me before and I have a certain level of trepidation in revealing it now. In truth, I worry for my own safety and hope that the passage of time minimises Karen's desire for vengeance. Nevertheless, it is a risk I have to take for the sake of full disclosure.

To safeguard against any potential retribution from my ex-wife, I recently sought out a gypsy fortune teller known to my deceased grandmothers and asked her for help. Because of the close ties she had with my Babas, the old crone gave me a talisman she swore was the petrified ring-finger of the Virgin Mary herself. She guaranteed any sorcerous attacks made by Screech would be deflected as easily as the Mother of Christ convinced the world her pregnancy was a result of immaculate conception and not a midnight rendezvous with her husband's brother. Looking back, it's unfortunate I did not possess this charm during the antenatal classes. If I did, Amelia Dyer's dark magics would have certainly been thwarted and she would have been starved.

The key to my plan was a cot in storage in one of my grandfather's sheds. This thing was ancient. It had first been used by my father and then myself. It was also coated in thick, lead-based paint. While the weak children of the west would have suffered health problems being exposed to this toxic coating, Slavs are made of sterner stuff and neither my sire or myself suffered any detrimental effects. However, as my children were not fortunate enough to be pureblooded Ukrainians, I needed to repaint the frame in weak, water-based pigments to better suit their compromised constitutions. Regardless, paint was a hell of a lot cheaper than buying a new cot.

The problem was, that even after I had finished restoring this crib, it still looked dated. To convince first, Screech, and then years later, Karen, to use this artefact of the past was going to be a big ask. There was still a chance though. While carrying a child, a woman becomes notoriously emotional. Consequently, family ties and traditions become very important to her. This was the Achilles Heel I needed to exploit.

With regards to Helga, my scheme came to fruition one Sunday while Screech and I were enjoying lunch at my paternal grandparents' home. We did this on a semi-regular basis and the meal never disappointed. It was always traditional Ukrainian fare: borscht, varenyky, stuffed cabbage, holodets and my favourite, piroshki, all cooked to perfection by Baba Chook. My grandfather, Did Chook, always brought out his homemade moonshine because a Ukrainian meal isn't complete without some hard liquor on the table. Ukes, like all Slavs, know how to put on a spread. If you have a friend with Eastern European heritage you need to invite yourself to a family feast. They are unsurpassed. Just remember not to smile.

Once again, I am sorry for diverging from the current discussion, but I love Ukrainian food more than Satan loves getting his butthole kissed at a black mass. It would be remiss of me if I failed to recommend that you, the reader, did not give it a try if given the opportunity. The food, not kissing the Devil's ass.

As stated, Screech and I were at Baba and Did Chooks' domicile enjoying a meal of unsurpassed excellence when I put my plan into action. I had two things in my favour:

Firstly, Screech was entering a torpor after consuming enough food to feed a small nation. As her hunger was sated, she was guaranteed to be more docile and open to suggestion.

Secondly, she could not speak Ukrainian and more importantly, my grandparents did not speak a word of English. Now when I say they didn't speak any English I don't mean that they couldn't. They had lived in Australia for around forty years by this time, so they had picked up enough of the native tongue to interact with society at large. As a matter of fact, Baba Chook was quite fluent. Nevertheless, they refused to speak anything other than Ukrainian when at home. Screech was ignorant of this fact and assumed that the only way she could communicate with Baba and Did was through me. This was a source of much amusement amongst the Chook clan.

After cleaning the food splatters from her face, hair, shirt and hands as best as she could, my increasingly hefty wife rummaged through her handbag. She eventually located a catalogue from some stupid fucking random baby supply store. I think they were called, "Sucks to Be You!", but I'm not one hundred percent sure to be honest. It doesn't matter, all those shops are the same. These scam artists are no better than lawyers, politicians, accountants or antenatal class instructors. They all seek to profit by exploiting the bewildered, unwary and emotionally vulnerable members of society. Screech flicked through the pamphlet until she found the page advertising cots and handed it to me. She pointed at the one that had been circled and hissed, 'Show Baba and Did the crib we're going to buy for Helga.'

I took the despised sales brochure from her, placed it in front of my grandparents and said, 'See this?' as I tapped the picture of the crib chosen by my wife.

'Do you see how much it costs? This is what she wants to buy for the baby. She's bat-shit fucking insane! I need to convince her to use the cot that I painted but you have to help me, okay?'

Remember that this was communicated in Ukrainian so Screech had no idea what I had just said. Baba and Did Chook nodded while grinning like idiots at the totally oblivious woman sitting next to me, who by this time was absently picking pieces of boiled cabbage from behind her ear and stuffing them into her mouth.

'What's the plan M'Lord?' my grandfather asked in the

language of our people as he poured both of us a shot of moonshine.

'I'm going to tell her that it's tradition for me to use the cot Dad and I slept in.' I replied as I accepted the proffered glass.

Now Slavic women have mastered the art of the guilt trip and can burst into tears at will, which Baba C promptly did while crying out in her native tongue, 'Yoi! Yoi! Yoi! Your wife is mad!' as she raised her face and outstretched arms to the heavens, 'Why waste money on a new cot when there is a perfectly good one here!'

Screech was obviously taken aback by my grandmother's outburst. 'M'Lord, what's wrong with Baba?'

I slammed back the fire water.

'She's upset that you won't use the cot me and my dad had.' I answered while pretending to console Baba, who was still wailing like a woman possessed.

I went on to explain how it is a Ukrainian tradition for me, the eldest son, to use the same crib for my spawn as was used by both my father and I, and that my Baba was obviously upset that we were not going to continue the custom.

'Do you think she's falling for it?' Baba Chook asked as she wiped away crocodile tears.

I looked at Screech and saw she was on the verge of crying.

'Without a doubt. Good work Fam.' I answered before downing another shot.

'What did she say?' my wife sobbed.

'That you will bring doom onto our child if you break the chain. They worry that Helga will be born with hideous deformities if we get a new cot."

Screech studied each of us in turn, searching for any sign in our expressions that would reveal our deception for what it was. To no avail. Unflinchingly, we all met her gaze, E.E.S. ensuring our faces were blank canvasses that revealed nothing except for the perpetual scowl that is common to those with the affliction. She took this as a sign of disapproval for even thinking about abandoning my cultural "traditions" and risking the wellbeing of our daughter. Reluctantly, she relented.

'Baba,' she said as she took my grandmother's hands into her own, 'We no buy cot OK. We take M'Lord's instead. No break tradition. You happy now, yes?'

Like all native English speakers that try to communicate with ethnics, my wife had resorted to baby speak. Why do you all do this? It beggars' belief. Talking like a "Playschool" presenter is not going to make you more intelligible. It makes you appear intellectually stunted. It is no wonder that the rest of the world considers the Anglo-Saxon race to be backwards. For the sake of your reputations on the global stage, fucking stop it.

Anyway, Baba Chook looked my wife in the eye and gently patted her on the cheek. She then glanced in my direction and said, 'M'Lord, why did you marry this one? Her head is empty. I swear she could be tricked into milking a bull.'

'What did she say Babe? Are they happy now?' Screech pleaded, her voice taking on a desperate tone.

I looked at my grandparents and gave silent thanks to my goat-headed Lord for their aid.

'Are they happy, she asks.' I remember thinking to myself, 'Who cares! I've just saved enough money to buy a new guitar!'

'Yeah babe, they're happy. Thank you.' I answered as I fed a varenyky I found on the floor into her gaping mouth.

Time passed and my union with Screech ended. I met Karen and she was instantly besotted with me. Unsurprisingly, we were wed and a few years later my new jailer, not satisfied with just being a stepmother, wanted to have a baby of her own. I was not as enlightened as I am now so I foolishly agreed. After all, it involved dancing the dance of love, of which I am a big fan. It didn't help that our families were pushing for us to have a child either. The bastards should have worried about their own backyards and kept their noses out of mine. At any rate, my off the charts sperm count meant it wasn't long before I had fertilised the egg that would develop into Mugwomp.

Days became weeks which became months and Karen grew and grew. It was like watching stop motion footage of a startled puffer fish. Eventually, her thoughts turned to Mugwomp's sleeping arrangements and the need to waste money. We urgently had to have "that talk" but this time, to my surprise, my grandparents took care of it themselves. I didn't have to do or say a thing.

Once again, we were at my grandparents' place, enjoying another Sunday lunch. By now Baba and Did Chook had dropped their charade and openly spoke to Karen in English. For some reason they loved this woman, as opposed to the disdain they held Screech in. I think it was because she was an actual human and not a fork tongued spawn of the pit.

'So M'Lord and I have been looking at cots.' Karen started to say as we gorged ourselves.

'Darling,' Baba Chook interrupted, 'Don't be silly. We have one already. M'Lord and his father both slept in it. Helga as well.'

'But it's so old Baba. I want a new cot for this baby,' my wife continued.

Did Chook, looked up from his glass, 'Yes is old. But is strong!' he boomed. His English wasn't as fluent as my grandmother's, so he spoke like a stereotypical Russian movie villain. 'And your baby no be broken.'

Karen looked confused by this. Her face took on a blank expression, like a dress mannequin.

'What Did means, is that it is tradition for the children of the eldest son to sleep in the cot of their father. To go against this is to bring down the wrath of the Old Witch!' my grandmother declared.

Baba had outdone herself. She had gone from the simple story we used on Screech to invoking a dark horror from Slavic myth. Baba Yaga, a monster that fed on children. This evil bitch was a source of absolute terror from my childhood, so I was curious to see where my grandmother was going with this. I poured myself a glass of Did Chook's finest and settled in for the show.

'Who?' Karen asked.

'Yoi! Yoi! Yoi!' Baba cried out. This was the traditional way for a Slavic woman to start any conversation of such gravitas, 'Baba Yaga! An evil witch that hungers for the flesh of young children. A bride of the Devil!'

My grandmother proceeded to cough up a wad of phlegm and violently spat it onto the ground, an act my grandfather imitated with much gusto.

'Baba, that's just a dumb superstition.' Karen interrupted, a look of horror on her face as she stared at the blobs of saliva glistening on the otherwise spotless kitchen floor.

'No! No no, no, no, no, no, no, no! No Karen! No!' Baba liked to make sure she got her point across, 'It's not superstition. No!'

'Darling,' my grandfather addressed my grandmother, 'tell them about your sister.' He looked Karen in the eye and banged the table to emphasise his point, 'Svetta having baby too. She think she trick Baba Yaga.' Both he and Baba Chook spat on the floor again.

'Ha! Yes, Svetta think tradition silly. No listen to husband's family. Think Baba Yaga is joke.' More spit. 'You know what happen? Was big trouble for...'

Before he could finish, Did Chook was cut off by Baba, 'Svetta was my eldest sister. A beautiful girl, like you Karen,' my wife blushed, 'but also like you she thought our traditions were silly. Well one autumn, a few years before the war, she was married to a farmer from the village. His name was Piotr. A handsome man. It was not long before she was with child.'

Baba paused her story while I poured my grandparents and myself another glass of Did's potent brew. We crashed our glasses together and downed the contents before I refilled them once more. Karen looked on with envy as she grudgingly sipped her water. She liked a drink before she got pregnant and missed the days of rolling down the road and throwing up in the back of cabs.

Now Baba was a tiny woman, not even five feet tall, and the drink was going to her head. She started getting more animated as she continued her tale.

'When our families found out Piotr and Svetta were going to have a baby there was a big party. The whole village celebrated. Music, dancing, singing, it was so much fun. And the drinking! So much drinking! You know, my father gave me my first glass of vodka that night. Oh my God it was like fire in my chest! But then it made me feel so good. I was the happiest seven-year-old in the world!' Baba stopped talking and her eyes teared up as she remembered a night that never even happened. She was the consummate fucking professional. Respect.

Karen was hanging on my grandmother's every word. Baba wiped the tears from her eyes, blew her nose and sighed, 'Such good times, now where was I? That's right. Everyone was having so much fun. I remember near the end of the night Piotr's parents presented him and Svetta with a crib. It was very old and in need of much repair. They told the assembled crowd that this cot had first been used by Piotr's grandfather, then by his father and finally by Piotr himself. As he was his parents' eldest son it was tradition that he used it for his own children.

'There was a murmur of approval from all of the guests as this was a well-known custom. Well, from everyone but Svetta. While she thanked her in-laws for the gift and appeared grateful, I knew my sister well. Our eyes met and I knew, even at that young age, that there was no way Svetta was going to allow her firstborn to sleep in that rickety old thing.

'Well, a few weeks later there was an "accident". Svetta told us all with mock sadness in her voice that while Piotr was repairing the cot in the barn, their plow horse was spooked and broke out of its stable. In his rush to catch the beast Svetta's husband knocked over a large pile of firewood that had been stacked for the winter. Unfortunately, this landed on top of the cot and smashed it to smithereens. We looked to Piotr for confirmation but all he did was nod while staring fearfully at my sister. Svetta told us that when they told his parents, Piotr's mother began crying out the name of Baba Yaga.'

Baba Chook's narration came to a halt yet again as she and Did both hawked up some more phlegm and spat on the floor for a fourth time. Not wanting to miss out on all the fun, I added a wad of my own saliva to the growing pool at our feet, much to Karen's disgust. Just like before, my grandmother continued as if nothing had happened.

'Piotr ended up building a new crib and it was beautiful. He had carved baby bears and birds into the frame and it was painted a lovely bright red.' She paused and began to sob gently, dabbing at her salty crocodile tears. Baba Chook was milking it for all she was worth.

'Months passed and the destruction of the old cot was forgotten. The time came for Svetta to give birth and both families were so excited to welcome the new baby into the world. Aieee! Karen, this day should have been a day of such joy but because my sister did not listen to her husband's family her poor baby was cursed by Baba Yaga!'

Cue three-way synchronised spitting. The amount of drool on the linoleum was turning the floor into a wading pool. It was disgustingly marvelous. This must be the reason many houses in the Ukraine still have dirt floors. Anyway...

'What was wrong with the baby?!' my emotional wife demanded as she stroked her swollen belly.

'YOIYOIYOIYOIYOIYOIYOIYOIYOIYOIYOIY OIYOIYOIYOIYOI!' Baba wailed.

'AAAAAAAAIIIIIEEEEEEEEEEEE!' Baba cried, tears and snot moistening her glorious moustache.

'Please tell me, Baba!' Karen implored, her own fragile emotions starting to get the better of her.

'Yoi my darling, Svetta's poor baby was born with the feet

and face of a rat!' my grandmother cried out before starting to sob uncontrollably.

Did Chook took this as his cue to get in on the action, and rose unsteadily to his feet, the homemade vodka going straight to his head as he stood. He began to stagger over to Baba to offer her comfort when he slipped in the massive puddle of drool and landed flat on his back. I had to excuse myself and go to the toilet before I burst into laughter and ruined all of my grandparents' hard work.

'Do you see Karen?' Baba sputtered as she composed herself, 'The Old Witch punishes us for trying to stop her curse!' She pointed at my grandfather struggling to get up as he kept slipping in the copious amount of saliva coating the kitchen floor. 'Please, you have to use M'Lord's cot or your child will suffer like Svetta's.'

It didn't matter how fucking ludicrous the story she had just been told was. Karen was a whirlpool of conflicting emotions. She knew it was impossible for a human child to be born with rat-like features. At the same time, she saw how impassioned Baba had become while reliving the fabricated horrors from her imaginary childhood. Seriously, my grandmother had missed her calling. She should have been a star.

I returned after composing myself and looked into my darling wife's tear-streaked face and knew victory was once again mine.

'M'Lord,' she sniffed, 'I've changed my mind. I don't want to upset Baba and Did any more.'

As I helped my grandfather regain his footing and eased him back into his seat, Karen poured the three of us another drink and proclaimed, 'Okay. I didn't realise how important this cot thing is to you guys. I'm sorry. M'Lord and I would be proud for Mugwomp to continue the family tradition.'

My grandparents clapped and cheered and we lucky three finished our drinks while Karen hydrated. As Baba came over and caught my wife in a huge embrace, she winked at me from over her shoulder while I gave her a big thumbs up.

The day came to an end and Karen helped me stagger to our car. She asked, 'So, babe, are you OK with using the old cot again? I know a new one would have been good but did you see how happy we made Baba and Did?'

I fell into the passenger seat, chuckled and slurred, 'Shit yeah, babe. I don't want no fucking rat faced kid!'

We still have that cot collecting dust in the shed, I shit you not.

2) The Rocking Chair

Let me make this perfectly clear. Rocking chairs have their place. That place is under the ass of an old lady knitting shit-brown cardigans. Or an old man on his porch yelling at the youth in his neighborhood for daring to tread on his finely manicured turf. They do not belong in a nursery patiently waiting to crush the hands of your curious little shit machine. Mothers the world over profess how they would lay down their lives to protect their children. The fact that they all seem to want one of these upon discovering they are pregnant indicates that this is a lie. Ladies, if you truly love your kids, don't buy a damn rocking chair. They are expensive, dust-collecting death traps. Leave them for those with one foot in the grave already.

I can't remember how, but when Karen was close to expelling Mugwomp from her innards she managed to get hold of one. Knowing her, she probably pilfered it from a nursing home she was working at. She's like that. The how's, why's and wherefore's are irrelevant. The fact of the matter is that I came home from work one afternoon and before I could even get out of the car, my wife waddled out of the house like Pooh Bear chasing a honey thief.

'M'Lord! M'Lord! I'm so glad you're home!' she exclaimed. She was so excited that her whole body quivered like a bowl of jelly.

'Oh, are you?' I asked lustily as I began to unzip my pants, ready to unleash "Mr Chuckles" once inside the front door.

'Not for that, you dickhead.'

Karen has such wonderful pet names for me.

Dejected, I forced my serpent-like appendage back into my trousers. Not an easy task when it was waking, even with two hands.

'So why are you so excited then?' I queried. The look in Karen's eye had me concerned. The Womb had acquired something.

'Come with me, babe.'

Karen took me by the hand and led me down the hall to Mugwomp's room.

'Have… a look… at… what… I… got!' With a flourish she opened the door like a magician revealing an empty compartment to a captivated audience. Except the compartment wasn't empty and I was far from captivated by my discovery.

In the corner of the room, under the window, was a rocking chair. Like an apex predator, it sat, motionless, waiting for the time to strike and kill its unwary prey.

'How much?' I asked.

'That's the best thing. I got it for free.'

'Really? That's pretty cool I guess. Who did you get it from?'

'Don't worry about it babe, it doesn't matter.' Karen's tone made it clear I wasn't to pursue the matter any further.

'Mind if I ask why? It's nice and all but what do we need a rocking chair for?' I knew the answer but I had to ask the question anyway.

Karen made her way over to it, 'So I can sit here during the day and feed little Mugwomp in the sun.'

The chair creaked in protest as my wife sat down. She started rocking enthusiastically and it began making the most horrendous squeaking noise imaginable. It was so bad that dogs from around the neighborhood started howling as their eardrums threatened to burst. Of course, Karen was intentionally oblivious to the tortured sounds emanating from beneath her padded ass and the streets outside.

'See? This will be so good for feeding.' she stated in a way that brooked no argument.

'And raising the dead.' I muttered to myself.

'What was that M'Lord?'

'I said I better go out to the shed.'

'Why?'

'To get some oil to stop that fucking squeak!'

'What squeak?' Karen enquired.

I stared at her incredulously as blood slowly seeped from my ears. 'You can't be serious! You've deafened every dog within half a mile.'

'Don't know what you're talking about babe. You must be hearing things.'

Karen has an infuriating habit of not being able to find

fault with anything she does or acquires, regardless of how obvious said fault is. To be honest this flaw in her character makes me want to end her at times. My fear of incarceration is the only reason that she still draws breath. That and my all-encompassing love for her of course.

I oiled every part on that rocker but it made no fucking difference. Even the slightest movement set it off. If Karen ended up using this chair for every feed, I would lose my mind. I begged her to get rid of it but she would not budge. As stated previously, what The Womb wants, The Womb gets. The only concession I managed to coerce from Future-Mum was that the rocker would stay in Mugwomp's room. This had more to do with the fact that Karen was unable to move it on her own rather than any empathy she felt towards me. Of this I was certain.

While I had resigned myself to life in a padded cell with rapey orderlies for friends, circumstances unfolded that allowed me to avoid that fate.

Once Mugwomp was born, had her horns filed off and been given the all clear to come home, Karen couldn't wait to start using the baby milkshake making machine. When she got that chair moving, I swear you could hear the tit juice sloshing about inside her breasts. It sounded like waves gently lapping against the hull of a boat and could almost have been pleasant if not for the noise produced by the chair itself. I was certain that if she rocked long enough, bubbles would start appearing from her nostrils as the milk frothed up inside her.

As it turned out Karen only ever used that rocking chair maybe half a dozen times. The pact I had made with my wife ensured that the infernal thing would remain in Mugwomp's nursery. It just so happens that this room was at one end of the house while the living room and entertaining areas were at the other end. Karen is a very social animal and being isolated from what was going on while feeding our darling little hellspawn was not going to be tolerated for any length of time. Within a fortnight of Mugwomp being born the rocker had been abandoned in favour of the lounge. The rocking chair had gone from pre-eminent feeding accessory to forgotten dust collector in less than fourteen days. It was as if it had never existed. Buried as it was under the piles of baby clothes and blankets, we never gave it a second thought. Just as it had planned from the very beginning.

A year and a half later Karen and I were jolted from our zombie like trance by a high-pitched scream of pain coming from our precious daughter's room.

'Mugwomp!' Karen wailed as she launched herself from her seat with a speed she hadn't achieved since before she was pregnant.

'That fucking rocking chair!' I cursed as I realised what had transpired. The consummate hunter that it was, the rocker had bided its time until the perfect opportunity to strike presented itself.

As I entered Mugwomp's nursery she held out her hand for me to inspect as she clung to her mother's neck with the other. I noticed two squashed fingers, one with a nail that was starting to blacken. Thankfully, nothing was broken. I gently kissed my girl's chubby little hand better and asked her what had happened.

With a look of hate Mugwomp pointed to the rocking chair, 'Bad chair!'

'Yes, it is, Muggy. Want me to get rid of it?'

'Yes, Daddy! Fwow away!' my girl answered while

nodding so vigorously I thought her head might detach itself.

My expression hardened as our eyes locked. 'What. Did. You. Call. Me?'

Mugwomp's mouth dropped open and her bottom lip began to quiver as she realised what she had just said. 'Sowwy, da- sowwy, My Ward. Pwees fwow away, My Ward.'

My daughter was still unable to pronounce the letter "L". I gave her a little smile and kissed her on the cheek as she hugged Karen close.

'Good girl,' I praised her, showing she was forgiven, 'I will take this nasty chair away and it will never hurt you again, okay?'

She grinned that cute yet hideous gap-toothed smile all toddlers have and clapped enthusiastically as I hefted the piece of shit chair out of her room and down the hall, cursing as I smacked my hands into the walls while it cracked my shins.

'FUCKING MOTHERFUCKEEEEEEEEEEERRRR!' I raged as I manhandled the damn thing out to the shed and dragged it into the corner where it would spend the next thirteen years, gone from both sight and mind.

That was when Karen had decided it was time we moved our family to a larger residence. While sorting through all the shit we had accumulated, it was inevitable this hated chair saw the light of day once more. We could have sold it but passing such evil onto others knowing what it was capable of would have been unconscionable. Instead, it was decided that we would end this cuntish thing then and there. Boris, (more on him later, suffice to say that he was around at this point in time), Mugwomp, Karen and myself armed ourselves with tools of righteous destruction and proceeded to turn the rocking chair from Hell into kindling.

I've said it before and I'll say it again. Rocking chairs are evil fucking sons of bitches. Do not get one. They are needed in your lives as much as children are.

3) Plastic Baths

Even though these things cost sweet fuck-all why would you bother getting one? Sure, if you live in a cave you may need somewhere to wash your filthy offspring but there is probably a stream nearby. Or you own a pet that keeps it clean. Either way, even if you are living in the most primitive manner, there are still better options. If you are civilised like the majority of us, then you have no excuse. Assuming that you live in a house, apartment or some other similar domicile then you should have access to a few alternatives.

The first comes as no surprise. That room you shower in? Guess what? Most of them have, wait for it, bathtubs. Imagine having a bath in a bathroom! Genius, I know. Even better, the bath in question is normally fairly big. Definitely big enough that you could bathe with your child at the same time. Not only do you get parent-parasite bonding time but you are also conserving water and doing your bit for Mother Earth. Good on you, you fucking tree-hugging hippie.

So you don't have a bath? Personal experience tells me it is possible to shower with your little cherubs. The results are the same as bathing together. If that doesn't take your fancy, may I draw your attention to the laundry. Chances are there is a rather large tub available for infant cleaning in here. Likewise, every kitchen I have ever been in has had a sink to wash dishes in. It can't be that much of a stretch of the imagination to consider cleaning bubs in the same sink, can it?

If you have a yard, you must have access to a hose. While

you could spray your kid down like a muddy hound all year round, the more compassionate parent would probably limit these hose-downs to the warmer months of the year. Before you condemn this method as a bit extreme can I just state that if it was good enough for John Rambo in "First Blood", then shit, it's good enough for a baby, isn't it? Water the lawn at the same time like a real eco-warrior.

Finally, if you have access to a pet dog, you also have access to the most ecologically friendly child cleaning option on the planet.

Some may argue that you need a plastic bath because its portability makes washing your child while visiting friends a breeze. I call bullshit. It's something else you need to transport when you go out and trust me, you will be taking enough already. Unless your hosts are sharing the cave with the neanderthal mentioned above they should have access to all the options you have in your own home. If they won't let you use their bath, sink, hose or dog then I would argue they are not friends at all. They are selfish pricks not worthy of your time and company. Scum like this should be excised from your life immediately.

If you still insist that a plastic bath is a necessity then please consider the material these things are made from. It's right there in the name: P... L... A... S... T... I... C. This crap is one of the major contributors of pollution in our oceans, rivers, atmosphere, fucking everywhere. It's suffocating the planet and buying a plastic bath makes you a part of the problem. Your kid won't care if it was washed in a sink when it was a baby, but will you be able to look them in the eye when the world they inherit from you is a poisonous shithole? Be a positive influence in your child(ren)'s lives.

There is only one reason to purchase a plastic bath. They make cheap cots.

4) Baby Clothes

I fully appreciate that we need to dress our children to protect them from the elements. Human young are weak, fucking useless lumps of meat. If exposed to extremes of hot or cold for any length of time an infant will die. Unlike the young of most other species that share this world, ours are totally ill-equipped for survival. They have no natural insulation, they are unable to move about on their own and to make matters worse they can't even communicate with their betters. Crying doesn't count as it's a crapshoot trying to work out what the little squealer's problem is. A human child is totally dependent on their parents for survival for the first twenty-seven years of life. That said, they are extremely useless from birth until they reach seven or so, when they can start contributing to their upkeep.

To be honest, it's a miracle that we as a species weren't wiped out at the dawn of time.

So it is understandable that we need to clothe our little bundles of joy. The problem is the amount of money The Womb wants to spend in keeping our offspring dressed. Babies and little kids grow reasonably fast. They are also spectacularly messy. Shitting, pissing, vomiting and drooling all over themselves constantly. Why then does Future-Mum feel the need to spend hundreds, if not thousands of dollars, on a fashion wardrobe the Kardashian family would be envious of? Everything your kid wears is either outgrown or destroyed within weeks of purchase. For Boris' first birthday and christening (we like to hedge our bets regarding the afterlife)

Karen bought him a tiny tuxedo to wear. While I admit he did look gangster as fuck, like a bobble headed Don Corleone, he only ever wore it one time. A waste of fucking money.

Even though the secondhand market for kids' clothes is massive and the daycare lost and found bin is a nice source for jackets and shoes, there are still way too many women spending large wads of cash on upmarket baby clothes. This is purely an attempt to outdo their friends at the play cafe.

These designer brands exist solely to stroke the vanity of wannabe influencer mums. You know the type. They all have stripper names like Mercedes, Desiree or Karen and are in debt to their eyeballs keeping up appearances. Fifteen-centimeter-long fake eyelashes and lips with so much filler they wouldn't seem out of place on a hippo's vagina are also the norm for these hooker lookalikes.

All these peacocks flock together and drink their Frappuccino fucking lattes, wasting their lives judging the rest of us that dare to dress our kids in Bonds babywear. All while their inbred offspring, gorgeous in the latest Dolce & Gabbana jumpsuits, roll around in their own shit and vomit. These mums need to wake up and stop supporting the sweatshops that produce the designer clothes they dress their little darlings in. Produced by kids not much older than their own young and in conditions that aren't exactly conducive to a child's development.

Even though they probably deserve it, child slavery is a stain on humanity and it needs to be stopped. As consumers we can help end it by changing our spending habits. If the demand for high street babywear disappears then those evil cunts that use child labour to make their garments won't have any reason to do so.

So c'mon Mercedes, c'mon Desiree, make a fucking difference.

If it was up to me, I would have dressed my three shit machines in biodegradable plastic bags. Cut some holes for arms and legs and you're ready to go. If you use a typical shopping bag you only need to cut leg-holes as the handles give you an instant pair of overalls. When the kid's waste inevitably breaches its nappy or it throws up all over itself, who cares. Rip off the soiled bag, bin it and while your loyal four-legged friend cleans up bubs you grab another bag, cut a couple of holes and your child is good as new.

As a bonus, the non-porous nature of plastic means your child's own body heat will keep it warm during cold weather. When it's hot and you feel the need to dress your kid in something (I don't understand why you would bother dressing little kids in summer but whatever, each to their own) just cut some more holes for increased ventilation.

In fact, if this book sells, the Understanding E.E.S. Foundation may well invest some of the proceeds into developing hemp based, biodegradable, plastic babywear that comes on a roll, just like garbage bags. Instead of a wardrobe and chest of drawers taking up space in the nursery all you would need to do would be to hang the roll of plastic clothes on the back of the bedroom door, just as you would a roll of toilet paper.

What a brilliant idea. At least I think so. Karen obviously thinks it is stupid but what does she know.

Footwear for infants is a whole other level of stupid. We all know babies can't walk. Whether because of some ancient genetic defect or because your God has a fucked-up sense of humour, human youngsters do not develop the motor skills or balance required to put one foot in front of the other and ambulate until they are around twelve months of age. So why buy them shoes? They have no need for them. Surely there are better things to spend money on; like rolls of biodegradable plastic clothing perhaps.

Even when they are walking there is no need to waste money on new footwear. Your child's feet are growing constantly at this age and they will outgrow their shoes well before they wear them out. Hand me downs are the obvious answer but give the following a shot. Trust me, you'll have a ball.

Go to where the little tit munchers congregate: play cafe's, swimming classes, Macca D's. Anywhere that it's a requirement for children to remove their footwear to play is ideal. Have a wander around. If you see any shoes that you like, just take them. It's that fucking simple. The original owner is probably close to outgrowing them anyway. For an added thrill try this in a shoe shop. Locate a parent with toddler in tow and discreetly shadow them. They will eventually find a pair of shoes that takes their fancy and will want their child to try them on for size. This is when you strike. As soon as the old pair of boots is removed grab them and run like fuck. The adrenaline rush you get fleeing from an enraged mother flanked by shoe salespeople is a bucket list moment everyone should experience at least once.

In summary, when it comes to clothing your young'uns just be smart. You don't need to spend big. Your kids won't know, but your bank account surely will.

5) Prams

Prams and strollers are fantastic. I'm not a fan of baby

slings or carriers that involve me lugging a small child on my chest like some mutated marsupial. The little beast can claw your face with impunity. There is also a high probability the filthy animal will regurgitate a gut full of slop onto your person, which is far from desirable, and due to its proximity to your ears, the risk of permanent hearing damage when it cries is very real.

Prams keep the devil child at a safe distance that prevents all of the above from occurring. They have spaces to carry nappy bags and all the other crap you have to bring with you when you go out with your progeny. Most importantly, they are essential if you are going to participate in the high-octane sport of Baby Demolition Derby, loved by fathers the world over. They are one of the few pieces of equipment used in child-rearing that gives more than it takes.

The problem lies in that many parents pick a pram as a status symbol, rather than buying one that suits their needs. Just like those clowns that buy massive 4WD wagons that have no intention of ever taking their vehicle anywhere that would require high ground clearance or all-wheel drive capabilities.

Why the fuck do you need this beast of a car if all you do is take the kids to school and sporting events, go shopping, or catch up with Sharon for a coffee and a chat? Most owners of these vehicles can't even park them properly and generally take up two spaces because they're fucking useless behind the wheel of a car. They block the fields of vision for the rest of us that drive normal sized automobiles and are generally the most obnoxious, self-entitled road users of the modern era. I compare them to the infamous Volvo drivers of the 1980's and 90's.

The only advice I can give to prospective parents when it

comes to picking a pram is think with your brain, not your dick or female equivalent and do not, under any circumstances, listen to The Womb. Pick one that is practical and suits your needs.

If you don't plan on taking your spawn on cross country runs or bush walks, then don't invest in the "Mega Fucking Off Road Delux 2000S" with all-wheel independent suspension. Your friends and the common man on the street won't be impressed by your extravagant pram. They will think you are a tool. You will struggle to get it down shopping aisles and loading it into the boot of your car will need an engineering degree. In fact, you'll probably need to get one of those massive trucks to fit the damn thing in. Coincidence? I think not.

So if you are ever in the position where you need to purchase a pram just remember this little rhyme and you can't go wrong:

"When you buy a pram,
Don't be a fool,
Take M'Lord's advice,
And it'll all be cool."

Peace out, Motherfuckers.

6) The Baby Monitor

I HATE these things. Useless pieces of shit. They have a couple of redeeming uses but these have no correlation with their intended purpose and I will mention them shortly.

When an infant cries, it is in no way a peaceful soothing sound. Far from it. Why then would we need a device that amplifies its godforsaken wails? If you can't hear your child singing the song of its people without assistance, I would suggest a hearing test. Babies are fucking loud.

I know the arguments for getting one. Karen used them on me when she bought one without my knowledge. Here they are and why I call bullshit.

"The monitor lets you hear the baby when you are in another room or outside."

Really Karen? As I've said before, when junior cries it is very loud. In fact, there are rumours North Korea is harnessing legions of newborns to create a devastating new sonic weapon. That's how loud they are.

There is not much chance you won't hear your little one when it starts demanding your immediate attention, regardless of where you are. And if there comes a time when you can't hear your baby, then honestly, who fucking cares? Let the little shit scream. Hopefully it damages its vocal chords, demanding beast that it is.

A newborn's inability to do absolutely anything means that we, as parents, are forced by law to meet minimum standards of care. However, there is no obligation for us to drop everything at the first squawk. They need to learn who really holds the power in the parent-parasite relationship. Remember this: a slave runs when his master calls while a king serves his people when it suits him.

Be a king, not a slave.

"The monitor will wake us when she stirs through the night."

No shit Sherlock but the kid will do this at any rate. Why is that, dear reader? That's right. Because a crying baby is always at maximum volume. You will wake instantly. All a baby monitor will do is ensure that you stay awake long after your little one has settled again, its belly full and ass cleaned.

This is because the monitor still transmits the sound of your child breathing, amplified to levels that replicate the apocalyptic rage of a hurricane. If you are as light a sleeper as I am then a bit of shut eye will be a thing of the past. You're better off having a nap in the same room as bubs because it will be quieter than putting your head down next to that damn speaker.

When you think about it, a baby monitor is the equivalent of that annoying fucking bell your sick spouse rings when he or she demands your immediate attention in the bedroom. I am no goddamn butler or palliative care nurse and I refuse to be treated as such by my leech-like offspring. Neither should you.

Your little nipple shredder will not die if it has to wait a little while to be fed or changed. After all, when they get older the little pricks are always making us wait. Waiting for their chores to be done. Waiting for them to get dressed. Waiting for them to get in the car. Waiting for them to get a job so they can live off their own coin. Waiting for them to move the fuck out so you can build that sex dungeon you've always wanted.

You get the picture. So let them wait every now and then. Remember, at this moment in their pointless existences, your offspring are totally at your mercy, not the other way round.

Their bodies are primarily composed of fat so they won't starve to death if they don't instantly latch onto a teat, be it the mother's or a bottle. If they have soiled themselves, it won't kill them to lie in it for a while. Hopefully the discomfort that the product of your loins feels makes them reflect on their utter uselessness. The shame that they should rightly experience may even provide the impetus for them to evolve from meat puppet into someone that begins to instill some measure of pride in its creators. As parents we can but hope.

Baby monitors come into their own when your children get older. There are two uses I have found for them, one funny as fuck and one extremely useful.

The first can provide you, as parents, hours of side-splitting amusement. Granted, this could be at the expense of your kid's mental wellbeing, but honestly, the joy you experience will be more than worth a couple of years of therapy for the apple of your eye. After all the crap you have gone through in the years leading up to this moment, you deserve this tiny slice of payback.

Hide the speaker component of the baby monitor somewhere in your little darling's bedroom. Ideally it should be out of sight and reach of your child. Burying it amongst all the shit they jam under their beds can work, as can putting it on top of a wardrobe behind whatever ceramic monstrosity your budding Picasso has recently painted. An even better spot is inside a box that has been resealed with tape and left in the corner. My personal favourite however, is to carefully open up the kid's most beloved stuffed toy, insert the speaker, ensuring it is carefully wrapped in stuffing, before expertly restitching the hole you made. Fair dinkum, for what you are about to do, this one works a treat.

Congratulations, you have just created your own little room of horrors. Whenever the urge grabs you, turn on the microphone and start speaking. I prefer to use death metal growls or reading verses from the Satanic Bible but that's because this is what makes me happy. Remember, this is all about you for a change. Do whatever rocks your boat.

You might want that big, stuffed Elmo to tell little Timmy how he needs to step up and stop being such a horrible little brat for his parents. Cool. Or how about the voices under the bed telling sweet Lucy if she doesn't start keeping her room clean Mummy and Daddy are going to die. Excellent. Whatever you do though, make sure it makes you laugh because your child's mind is going to be messed up. All of a sudden, the room your mini-me has played and slept in, its sanctuary, has become a source of terror and that is going to fuck with their heads in some way. But you know what, in all honesty they had it coming. Oh yes, for everything they have done and everything they have yet to do they fucking had it coming.

It's up to you at what age you start this little game, but I suggest waiting until your young'un has started walking. The sight of your screaming toddler barrelling out of their bedroom and slamming into the wall like an out-of-control Teletubby is to die for.

I couldn't tell you the number of times I have had to stifle laughter as I searched through the rooms of my frightened offspring to show there was nothing to be scared of.

'It's just a bad dream Helga/Mugwomp/Boris. You're just imagining things. Now go to sleep.' I would say to them as I headed back to the living room where Karen was struggling to breathe through her tears and snot, such was the mirth she felt. Then we would wait a few minutes before I said something like, 'I told you not to tell Mummy and M'Lord about us! This is your last chance! Understand child?'

Oh, the memories. They give me tingles.

The other use for these devices is why I believe they were originally invented. To monitor your older children. You simply reverse your deployment of the monitor's components and hide the microphone in a discreet location. Sure, they are big and noticeable, especially compared to modern surveillance devices but today's teens are pretty stupid and the fact that their attention is constantly focused on a phone, game console or laptop makes hiding the mic a simple exercise. You just need to ensure that you put it somewhere they will never look. As with younger children, on top of the wardrobe or underneath their beds are both sterling locations.

Nothing they do will be hidden from you again. Like the Gestapo or KGB, you will be your family's own secret police, tasked with ensuring the family unit is not undermined by your rebellious offspring.

A word of warning though. Children at this age are massive hormone factories and are prone to random acts of masturbation. These can happen at all hours of the day or night, especially with regards to the male of the species. They cannot leave "Mr. Chuckles" alone for more than a few minutes at a time.

In the interests of your own mental wellbeing and so you can still look your kid in the eye, if you start hearing grunting or moaning turn the speaker off straight away. Some things are just not meant for a parent's ears and your teenager's wanking noises most definitely fall into this category. Remember that which has been heard cannot be unheard.

7) Toys

There isn't much advice I can give here. Even I wouldn't

deny a child's right to playtime but just remember, a newborn cannot do anything so there is no need to go overboard. A teddy and musical mobile above their plastic cot-bath is all they need for the first couple of months. Notice I said "*a* teddy" and "*a* mobile". Singular. There is as much need for multiple stuffed animals and circling butterflies as there is for the kid in the first place. Tell your friends and relatives to hold off on buying any toys as well or you will be inundated with boxes of shit that will never see the light of day. If they want to buy any gifts for your newborn, advise them to keep an eye out for something useful. Like a bottle of tequila.

 Once your little monster has developed some form of self-awareness, I strongly recommend getting a Jolly Jumper. Not one of the modern ones that come with their own frame. Those are for pussies. Track down an old school one that you attach to a door frame. These things fucking rock. All my kids loved the one we had. I would tie them in and pull them back until the springs were at maximum stretch and then let them go. The little bastards would hurtle down the hallway like a bullet! A favourite game of ours would be to wait for Karen to come through the front door & I would launch my mini human cannonball at her. The kids and I loved it. Karen, not so much. Especially when I had the rider wear a motorcycle helmet.

 Finally, if at any time someone buys your child any type of noisy toy you need to cut those people off. After punching them in the mouth. When they bought your kid that drum set it wasn't in the hope of developing any latent musical talent. Their first thoughts when they saw it in the shop was how much it was going to piss you off. I know because that is exactly what I am thinking when I buy gifts for any little kid that isn't my own. This is why Karen stopped me buying presents for our friends' offspring when they were little. I went out of my way to buy toys that would annoy the parents. For example, if I knew the mother and father were pacifists, I would buy their little one the best fucking toy gun I could get my hands on and I would make sure I gave it to the kid personally so Mum and Dad couldn't hide it away.

People like me take great pleasure in other people's suffering. You don't need that in your life.

Conclusion

There are many pitfalls for bewildered and unwary parents when it comes to preparing for a child's arrival. This chapter covers most of the major buying decisions that will be made and shows there are many viable alternatives that will save you money and a whole bunch of blood, sweat and tears. Just remember not to listen to The Womb. Like Jon Snow it knows absolutely fucking nothing.

Chapter 3:
What Annoyed Karen When She Was Pregnant

It would be remiss of me if I failed to devote part of this book to the things that aggrieved Karen, my beloved wife and (step)mother of my children. After much pestering due to her procrastinating nature, she finally presented me the following list:

The top 10 things that annoyed Karen when she was pregnant.
1) M'Lord's breathing
2) M'Lord's face
3) M'Lord's presence
4) M'Lord's absence
5) M'Lord's silence
6) M'Lord speaking
7) M'Lord sitting
8) M'Lord walking
9) M'Lord eating
10) M'Lord sleeping

Karen's list was much longer but for the sake of brevity this will suffice. You get the idea.

I've devoted enough space to her venomous ramblings.

She can write her own fucking book if she needs to vent. That's right, she can't, as she's borderline illiterate. Oh well, sucks to be her.

Conclusion.

Quite clearly, if rather unjustly, my bitch of a wife has identified me as the primary source of her grief while she was incubating Mugwomp and Boris.

Well Karen, fuck you.

Chapter 4:
It's on Its Way… Or Is It?

You may recall in Chapter One I was critical of the need for ante-natal classes that guided us through the signs and stages of labour. For those of you that suffer from goldfish brain here is a recap of what was asserted:

"To be honest this class was very informative. I hope that I remember everything that I learnt when I too am heavy with child. What a joke.
Sorry but if a woman can't tell when her body is about to spit out a sprog then I seriously doubt she should be having one in the first place. Have you experienced sudden, explosive fluid loss from your nether regions? Are you suffering from periodic abdominal pain that increases in frequency, intensity & duration? It could be gastro, but if you've been pregnant for around nine months then chances are you are going into labour. Have fun."

While this holds true the majority of the time, on occasion the little human wannabe is known to deceive its parents with a phenomenon known as Braxton Hicks contractions, more commonly known as false labour pains. Yet more proof that the little parasites will try and fuck with you any chance they get. Braxton Hicks contractions are just a sign that the unborn child has a truly malicious soul. These kids are destined to be a blight on humanity, more than any other. You may think this is hyperbole, an exaggeration, but it most definitely is not. I know it for fact as my second-born child, Mugwomp, put Karen through false labour and mark my words, she is a Herald of the Apocalypse.

A week or two before she came into the world Mugwomp decided it was time to show her true colours. Before the scene is set, be aware that the following is a tale cobbled together from sources other than myself. I was in no fit state to recall the events of that night. Nevertheless, what is recorded below can be considered gospel. Every. Last. Word.

It was a hot summer evening and I was having a few pre-emptive V.E.D. drinks with my brother from another mother, a man known as the Hermit.

I sense your confusion dear reader, "What the hell is this V.E.D.?" you're asking yourself. Worry not, you'll find out soon enough. Now is not the time.

As I was saying, The Hermit and I were enjoying a few beverages and bongs, soaking up the last of the daylight savings sun. When I say a few drinks, I was well on my way to hammer-town. I was loving life. Karen was sitting with us, but she was unusually surly, due to her being at the end of her pregnancy tether and not being able to partake in the festivities herself. She wasn't bringing much to the table to be honest.

In all fairness though, she couldn't be blamed. After months of constant growth, swollen ankles, sore back, crushed bladder and general discomfort, Karen had had enough. Mugwomp had overstayed her welcome and needed to get the fuck out.

All pregnant women eventually reach this point, some

sooner than others. Some women are pathetic and have had enough after a couple of months. To these I say harden up, bitches, the ride's only just begun. Then you have true champs of the pregnancy game, the Incubators of Legend like my mighty womb warrior, Karen the Insufferable. Up until the last month of her pregnancy she took everything in her stride. It didn't matter to her that she was so big she could be seen from orbit. She even put up with all the bullshit, inane comments thrown her way. You know the ones:

"Not long now."

"You sure it's not twins?"

"Pregnancy suits you."

"Look at you! You're glowing!"

Etcetera, fucking etcetera.

Before proceeding I feel a Community Service Announcement coming on.

If you're one to make such statements, do the mother-to-be a favour and just don't. The poor woman has heard them twenty times that day already. Give her a break.

And while I'm on my soapbox if you are one of those strange people that feels the need to rub a pregnant lady's belly you need to stop that right now. If you are not the foetus's father, sibling, grandparent, aunt or uncle you need to keep your hands to yourself. Even then it's best to ask first. Fucking weirdo belly touching motherfuckers. Cut that shit out.

I make no apologies. That needed to be said.

Karen, champion that she is, took all this and more in her stride until she was around eight months into her sentence. By that time, she wanted the whole pregnancy gig over and done with. I swear to God, at one point I had to coax her down from a tree she was threatening to jump out of in the hopes of inducing labour. This desire to have our offspring removed from her insides coincided with a souring of her demeanor. Karen was becoming positively hostile towards me. As it turned out, dangerously so. But like I said it was not her fault. The blame for what happened that night lay squarely with Mugwomp the Unborn.

So there we were, Karen, the Hermit and myself. As it grew dark, we ventured inside to escape the unwanted attentions of the waking mosquitos. I was so drunk that I passed out not long after sitting on the couch. The Hermit, opportunist that he was, took this as his cue to have some fun at my expense. First came the liberal application of makeup, then the obligatory cocks drawn on my forehead and cheeks. Finally, a flowery summer scarf and sombrero completed the look. It should be noted that while there is no proof to show her participation, at the very least Karen provided the makeup and was an amused bystander that actively encouraged my defilement. The selfies that were taken prove this.

It was at this point in time that Mugwomp decided to play her hand. There I was, looking like a drag queen hooker passed out on a park bench. I couldn't have been more vulnerable. And my unborn devil spawn decided to start playing games.

One contraction. Karen tentatively grabs her grotesquely swollen stomach.

Two contractions. She stares at me, storm clouds gathering above her head as I lay there, oblivious to the world around me. The Hermit was neither oblivious or a fool and he wisely put distance between himself and my comatose form.

After the third contraction finally hit all hell broke loose. Thanks a fucking lot, kid. Not even breathing oxygen yet and she was already making my life hell.

Karen unleashed a verbal tirade that would make Satan blush. The Hermit quoted her as screaming something along the lines of, 'FUCKING DBYFHDT NJXYDHUCBFJ UCFJNCM! M'LORD YOU ARE A FUCKING RJDHDUHCN UNHBCUJMN UJMNXBY FHCFCYN! I'M GOING INTO LABOUR AND YOU'RE PASSED OUT DRUNK YOU FUCKING SNRUBHDRUH DNXUH CBBDTYKGILKDUYH! WAAAAAAAAAAAAAGGGGHHHHH!
ARSEHOLE!'

None of this even registered in my pickled brain. I was that out of it you could have beaten me and I wouldn't have felt a thing. My lack of response to her righteous tongue lashing caused my darling wife to do just that. She straddled me and began beating my chest and slapping my face like I was a human drum kit.

'WAKE UP YOU BASTARD!' Karen raged as she abused my unconscious body.

I was informed that was the last legible sentence my long-suffering wife spoke that night. What came spewing out of her mouth next was nothing more than hate made manifest.

'CUNT CWTEVGHBT ULCYKM JNDVRSGDGX USELESS OKIUJHYGF GOAT FUCKER REFG SCRRRRRRRRAAAAAAAAAAAAAAAAAAAARRRR RRRRRRRRGH COCKSUCKERRRRRRRRRR!'

Pure vitriol poured from Karen's soul like oil from a ruptured fuel tanker on pristine arctic snow.

I remained insensible to my surroundings.

Mugwomp decided to up the ante.

A fourth contraction wracked my wife's body. Things were about to get real.

Before the cramping had even stopped my gorgeous Valkyrie of pain had dismounted me and stormed out of the room, continuing to spit curses at me all the while. The Hermit described her as a majestic blend of an obese She-Ra: Princess of Power and Regan MacNeil from "The Exorcist". I was in no condition to doubt him. He proceeded to describe, how not long after she stormed out of the living room, he heard drawers being opened and slammed shut in the kitchen. Then there was a period of total silence before heavy footfalls could be heard pounding down the hallway. Karen reappeared at the doorway. Although she was clutching an oversized wooden spoon in her hand, she had composed herself and her urge to inflict pain on me had passed.

Then I started snoring like an out-of-control freight train.

Just as my wife was gripped by a fifth contraction.

As you can imagine this pushed her over the edge.

'RRRRRRRRAAAAAAAAAAAAAAAAAAAAAAA RRRRRRRRRRRRGH!' she cried from the depths of her clogged up bowels as she brought the spoon crashing down onto my unprotected head.

As well as cursing me with the Eastern European Smile, my genes have gifted me with an exceptionally hard skull. The spoon had no chance and snapped in two after the first strike. If it wasn't for the Hermit dragging Karen off me, I am certain she would have rammed the splintered handle up my nose and into my brain.

And through all of this abuse I slept on, waking the next morning totally ignorant of the violence inflicted upon my person. If Karen and the Hermit hadn't informed me of the events of the previous evening, I would have been none the wiser.

Fortunately for me, the labour pains my daughter was inflicting upon my homicidal wife proved to be nothing more than a twisted game she was playing at my expense. She stopped once she realised Karen had finished beating on me. You may think I'm delusional but think on this you flock of naysaying bastards:

1) Mugwomp did not come into this world until a week after her due date and even then, Karen had to be induced to force our little Satan to evacuate the womb.

2) Karen never experienced any further contractions until V.E.D. (be patient, all will be explained in the next chapter).

These two points clearly show that even while gestating, my daughter's primary objective in life was to cause as much torment on her undeserving parents as possible. That she chose to first reveal her nature by inflicting false labour pains on my emotionally fragile wife was bad enough. The fact that Mugwomp did this while I was at my most vulnerable conclusively proves the statement made earlier that, "Braxton Hicks contractions are just a sign that the unborn child has a truly malicious soul."

Prove me wrong.

Conclusion.

Rather than recap what has been stated ad nauseum that children aim to break us, even before they enter the world, I can serve a higher purpose by helping partners of expectant mothers avoid my fate. Even though the traumatic experiences detailed above were one hundred percent my unborn daughter's fault, if I hadn't been paralytic then the night would have turned out differently.

If I was sober when Mugwomp started messing about, I could have been there to help Karen through an obviously scary time. Rather than being an object of hate, my wife would have seen me as a bedrock of support. I would have been capable of providing comfort, and if the contractions turned out to be the real thing rather than the evil torments of a soulless meat puppet, I would have been able to get Karen to hospital. As partners of expectant mothers, this is our only real job for the whole pregnancy. Get that moaning bitch to the hospital. Stat. One job and I could have messed it up royally.

What's worse is Karen still drags this up even now, eighteen fucking years later, in an attempt to belittle me in front of friends and family. I fucked up. I know it, she knows it, and now every one of you know it. Karen, if you ever read this, please, for the love of all that is heavy metal, give it a fucking rest.

Do I ever drag up the time she tried to run me over in her car? No, I don't. At least not until the next book.

So, birthing partners of gravid beasts everywhere, heed this advice above anything else presented in this manuscript. When the mother of your child is close to term, do not, under any circumstances, get fall-down drunk. The child in that woman's belly is waiting for any chance to mess with you so don't give it an opportunity to cause you grief. It will have time enough for that when it is born.

Which conveniently brings us to...

Chapter 5:
V.E.D.

The time has finally come for me to reveal the meaning behind that mysterious acronym that has occasionally cropped up in the preceding pages.

'Yeah, what the hell does V.E.D. mean, M'Lord?' I hear you ask.

Prepare to be enlightened.

The unwashed masses of humanity use the term "childbirth" to describe the event where your progeny finally enters the world. I prefer something less mundane. "Childbirth" makes the whole process sound far less traumatic than it actually is. Anyone that has experienced a child being born, be it as an active participant, observer, or even via the medium of television, knows it sure as hell isn't rainbows and fucking unicorns. It's a crazy ride of pain, shit and blood punctuated with a soundtrack reminiscent of a slaughterhouse. With all three of my kids I remember, even now, the howls and moans of pure agony coming not just from my wife, in the case of Karen, but from all the other occupied rooms in the hospital birthing suite. It was a true symphony of the damned.

No, "childbirth", "labour" and "delivery" have never conveyed the gravitas of the situation. I needed something more appropriate, so, in my infinite wisdom, I coined the term V.E.D.

Vaginal Expulsion Day. It's ugly, but so is birth. I even use it when my friends are celebrating the day they became a burden on their parents and society at large. Where others would say "Happy Birthday!" I wish them a Happy Vaginal Expulsion Day.

There you have it. Nothing earth shattering.

Before continuing into the meat of this chapter I need to make a confession. I find new-borns of the human variety ugly as fuck. There is so much propaganda professing the angelic beauty of freshly expelled infants, that we as a society have become brainwashed into actually believing the hype. Wake up sheeple and have a close look when you first lay your eyes on a recently born baby. Don't use the rose-tinted lenses imposed on you by popular ideology but look with the eyes of the enlightened.

Look real fucking close.

The act of passing through a hole many times smaller than what is required causes the head of a child to be compressed into a shape that is hideous to look upon. Even once all the blood, shit and other placental matter is washed off of the beast it is still unsightly. They look more like a misshapen ball of plasticine than something from the gene-stock of the homo-sapiens species.

Most outgrow this stage and end up looking passably human, but unfortunately, some retain these revolting facial features for the rest of their miserable lives.

Horror aficionados may recall a film from the eighties called "Ghoulies". The antagonists in this movie are baby-sized demons which cause all manner of torments on humanity once the gates of Hell are opened. These creatures are truly repugnant. Just like our young. Don't believe me? Google screen shots taken from this film, or even better track a copy down and watch it. Now compare these images with baby pictures. The similarities are uncanny.

Baby humans are repellently vile to look upon. This is fact. Deal with it.

Now back to the story at hand.

As V.E.D. is experienced differently by everyone that goes through it, I won't provide generic descriptions of what will be endured. Instead, I will take you through each of the three expulsions I have had the displeasure of attending.

Helga's V.E.D. (The V.E.D. That Wasn't)

Technically Helga, my first-born, wasn't so much expelled as she was extracted. Due to potential complications, my first wife, Screech, was to undergo a caesarean section. My disappointment was tangible.

I had attended those thrice cursed antenatal classes, put up with the mood swings and served as a maître d' to the miserable wretch, ensuring all of her unnatural cravings were met at all hours of the day and night.

And for fucking what?

My dreams of wallowing in Screech's reptilian hisses of pain were crushed. Vengeance for all I had endured would not be mine and I was gutted. My first wife knew it as well and wore her smugness like a cloak.

C-sections take all the random fun out of V.E.D. There is no sudden bursting of the dams when Future-Mum's waters break. (Honestly, it is amazing the amount of fluid that is discharged from a woman's nether regions when this happens. I believe the Judeo-Christian God took inspiration from this phenomenon for his Great Flood debacle.) You don't get to make a frenzied dash to the hospital with your groaning wife in tow, overnight bag clutched in her clammy mitts. Most importantly, your young one's arrival into the world is predetermined.

A natural birth can take hours of grunting, crying and abuse before your baby decides to reveal itself. Some women are so lazy or their young are so obstinate that it can take days before the child is expelled from its incubator. Meanwhile we, the long-suffering partners of these behemoths can finally take solace in the fact that we do not have to experience the ecstasies of birth ourselves. After months of demands and bullying at the hands of our significant other, we can finally put our feet up and relax while they do all the hard work. At most we need to let our loved one hold our hand, provide the odd word of encouragement and feed them a steady supply of ice chips.

Caesareans take this reward away from us.

Helga's arrival into the world was cold and clinical, robotic even. Just like her mother.

We arrived at the hospital and were led into a sterile room where Screech changed into a surgical gown. It was then that the Fallen Angel chose to smile upon his faithful servant. Even though the full V.E.D. experience was denied to me, there was still a consolation prize. Screech wasn't going to get out of it scot-free. She had to have an epidural, otherwise known as a spinal block. While the procedure isn't painful in itself, the sight of this big ass needle being driven into her spine soothed my sadistic nature somewhat. The past nine months hadn't been a complete waste of my time.

Then we were taken into the operating theatre and a few discreet scalpel cuts later, my firstborn, Helga, erupted into the world in a shower of crimson gore. That was it, all over. A bit of an anti-climax in my opinion.

Two stars. Do not recommend. While Helga's entry into the world was a joyful, momentous event in my life, the manner of her arrival left much to be desired. If she wasn't my firstborn, I would have rated this experience much lower on the scale.

Mugwomp's V.E.D. (Lights! Camera! Action!)

Of all the V.E.D.'s I have attended, Mugwomp's was the most fun by far. As it coincided with my thirtieth birthday celebrations, (Mugwomp was born a day after my own Expulsion Day Anniversary), it was a crazy time for everyone involved.

You may recall from the previous chapter it was mentioned that my darling little squatter ended up exceeding her welcome by a week. By this time Karen was beside herself and not just because she was so big it looked like there were two of her. She wanted Mugwomp out. Fucking yesterday.

As per the doctor's instructions Karen was admitted to hospital the day before she was to be induced. Note that this was the actual day I turned thirty. The dilemma I was faced with was not unlike that faced by President Truman in 1945 when he ordered the deployment of the first atomic bomb against the Japanese city of Hiroshima. Like Truman, my intent was to limit the loss of human life. Namely mine.

Fortunately, I had learnt my lesson. Where I would have normally celebrated my V.E.D. in glorious, debauched fashion, this year I limited my alcohol intake to around a dozen ales. While this may seem a significant quantity of beer by weak Anglo-Saxon standards, remember, I am a Slav.

Generations of alcohol abuse by my ancestors has gifted me with an iron liver. A dozen beers doesn't even register beyond a mild buzz and hangovers are not something I am familiar with.

My decision let me celebrate my thirtieth year, albeit in a more subdued manner than I am accustomed, and still be alert and ready for Mugwomp's forced eviction the following day. The big celebration was happening the day after Karen was liberated of her burden anyway, so I wasn't really sacrificing anything by being responsible (Christ I hate that word). As expected, I awoke bright and early and made my way to the hospital and Karen. And her mother. And her father.

As it was my wife's first child, and the first grandchild for her parents, Karen wanted them in attendance. Her mother, Mil, had spent the night at the hospital while her father, Longshanks, flew in from Queensland that morning. Even though her parents were separated, they were on good terms so it wasn't the shit-show that you may have expected. We said our hello's and I took my place at Karen's side.

While we waited for the doctor and midwife to show up and get the ball rolling, we were subjected to the wails of at least three other women in various stages of the labour process.

'AAAAAWOOOOOOOHAAAAAAAAFAAAAARK!'
'SHITARNNNNNNAAARRRRRYAAAAAAAAEEE!'
'RRRRRRNNNNGHAAAMAKEITFUCKINGSTOP!'

I found the whole thing hilarious. Karen most definitely did not. Each scream caused her to squeeze my hand to breaking point. She was fair dinkum shitting herself.

Finally, the professionals arrived and the day's adventure could begin. Karen prostrated herself on the bed and the doctor proceeded to examine her. Longshanks, not comfortable with seeing his daughter in such a compromised situation, discreetly left the room and wouldn't be seen again until his granddaughter had arrived. Mil, the stereotypical mother-in-law, wasn't going anywhere and would be with us for the long haul. Satisfied that everything was in order, the doctor left us in the care of our midwife, who would be responsible for inducing Karen.

Now would be the time to mention that I had recently come into possession of a video camera. It was my intention to record Mugwomp's expulsion for posterity. However, rather than film my wife's pained facial expressions and make inane commentary on a family-friendly vom-fest, I was going to take inspiration from Nurse Dyer's birthing video. This film was going to be honest and raw. It was going to be my magnum opus to cinema, a tribute to the horrors of childbirth.

The process of induction appears to have been ripped straight from the torture chambers of the Spanish Inquisition. First a long, green plastic rod that ends in a vicious hook was jammed into my wife's love tunnel. The purpose of this instrument was to perforate the amniotic sack, causing Karen's waters to break.

Our midwife was obviously new to her job and her skills left much to be desired. Five attempts later and she still hadn't been able to make the fluids flow. What was worse, this sorry excuse for a nurse was causing Karen significant levels of discomfort. I felt it was time to intervene. I handed Mil the camera and scrubbed up. As I pulled on a pair of blue latex gloves I bumped the amateur medico out the way, inserted my arm into my suffering wife, and with the expertise of a man who knows his way around a woman's vagina, instantly caused the waters to stream from her like a torn bladder of cask wine.

This is obviously utter bullshit and never happened but it's much more interesting than the reality. In actual fact the midwife called our doctor back and she took care of the job. See? That's boring as fuck so I'm playing the artistic license card and going with my version of events. After all, one should never let the truth get in the way of a good story.

As the waters gushed from Karen like a broken dam I turned to the midwife and asked, 'So, you think you can manage the rest?'

I removed the gloves with a snap and dunked them into the bin.

'M'Lord, that was amazing.' she responded, in awe of my skills.

'I know.'

I grabbed the dumbstruck midwife by the shoulders, looked her in the eye, and stated, 'Answer the question, woman, can you take care of the rest?'

She nodded sheepishly and slapped the magic ointment that would kick start the contractions into Karen's birth canal.

'Well, that should get the party started.' she mumbled as she left the room.

'I should fucking hope so.' my wife moaned.

About half an hour later the contractions began.

Now, Karen is hard as nails and had declined the offer of an epidural or any other type of pain relief. When that first contraction hit though, it made her eyes bulge like Arnold Schwarzenegger's in "Total Recall". The ones that followed only increased in both frequency and intensity and no matter what she did, nothing brought her much relief for any significant period of time.

Here are Karen's thoughts, in her own words, regarding drug-free methods employed by Future-Mums in an attempt to ease the uncompromising agonies inflicted by labour. These will be accompanied by a commentary from yours truly:

Lying Down: "At least no energy is required. If you are going to be in pain you may as well not be doing anything. Three stars."

While other positions might be explored, no doubt to get some sort of utility from birthing classes so they weren't a total waste of time, the vast majority of expectant mothers will revert to the old faithful. Flat on their back, cursing the man and child that put them in this sorry predicament in the first place. Karen's favourite pastime is sleeping so lying on a bed came naturally for her.

Sitting on a Chair: "Fuck no! This stops the whole process! Zero stars. Do not recommend."

There isn't anything I can add to this. Succinct and to the point.

On all Fours: "Crawling around on the lounge in the waiting room helped for a short while. Two stars."

This looked pretty damn funny. I think Karen felt a little like Simba from "The Lion King". My video footage shows she was more like Gloria from "Madagascar".

Standing: "Don't bother. The high energy requirement just isn't worth the benefit of using gravity. Besides, the baby may fall out and hit its head on the ground. One star."

All valid points, but in actual fact Karen is a sedentary

beast at the best of times, so standing was never going to be high on her list of things to do during labour. More active Future-Mums may find this option useful, especially if combined with a skipping rope. Remember to have something soft positioned underneath the mother in case the spawn suddenly pops out.

Squatting on the Toilet: "This is pretty comfortable, especially as giving birth feels a lot like being constipated. Three stars."

Is it a coincidence that having a baby feels like taking a shit and raising a child is the shittiest time of your life? I think not.

In the Bath: "While I never spent much time in the bath, because I was too frightened I'd end up swimming in shit and other body waste, I loved sitting in a hot shower. Probably my favourite place during labour. Five stars."

I have two theories as to why Karen found the shower so beneficial. Firstly, the steady stream of water hid her tears of regret. Secondly, the scalding heat was a source of comfort to my unborn child. This was because it raised my wife's core body temperature to levels more reminiscent of the fires of Hell from whence my daughter came. Her familiarity with the infernal temperatures that my wife found solace in meant Mugwomp was more placid than would have otherwise been the case. This in turn reduced the severity of the contractions inflicted upon Karen as my daughter was in a state of unholy bliss and less inclined to cause pain to her birth-giver.

On a Yoga Ball: "I was too fucking big and uncoordinated to balance on the damn ball. While it's cushioning under my fat butt was nice it was more satisfying to hurl it at M'Lord's head. Two stars."

I concur wholeheartedly with my love. Like so many women at full term, she had the coordination of an inebriated panda. Surprisingly her accuracy was unaffected and I was knocked on my ass a few times by both Karen and Mil when my filming became too intrusive for their liking. That was the price I had to pay for my art, but it was all worth it for the acclaim I was to receive from my captivated audience in the not-too-distant future.

Essential Oils and Incense: "A nice idea in theory but in practice a waste of time. Didn't do a fucking thing except mask the stench of stale sweat and shit. One star."

Spot on. I couldn't have said it better myself. A waste of fucking time indeed. Hippy crap.

Massage: "Nice for short bursts as it eased my back and shoulders but it didn't do anything for the contractions. Two stars but only 'cos my mum was there to do it. M'Lord massages like an epileptic gorilla."

As a trained masseuse, this was Mil's sole reason for being present at Mugwomp's expulsion day. At least she was good for something other than constantly adjusting her ample bosom. Seriously, the woman is Australia's answer to Dolly Parton.

Prayer: "What fucking good is prayer?! When you're in the throes of labour no God can save you. If God gave a shit, he would have had us lay eggs, not spit out a creature ten times too big for its exit hole. Zero goddamn stars."

Note these are Karen's words, not mine, but I agree with her one hundred percent. On the massive assumption that God actually exists, He must be a sadist of the highest order to make such a momentous occasion as childbirth be associated with so much suffering. Make no mistake either, your God is male. A female deity would have made sure males were the ones to go through the horrors of V.E.D.

Needless to say, my wife soon decided that she needed to take something to ease the pain. As I was to discover, the birthing suite was equipped with on tap laughing gas (how cool is that?) so Karen put on a mask and started sucking that nitrous oxide down like she was smoking the finest Lebanese Blonde hash. While it did help ease her agonies somewhat, it also made her feel quite ill. So much so that after a few tokes she was undecided as to whether she wanted to partake of the gas any more.

'Hey, babe, how you doing?' I began, gently stroking Karen's clammy forehead while she crushed my other hand.

'Amazing M'Lord.' A pause as she grimaced, 'How do you think, you fucking moron!' she spat, in the grips of another contraction

There she goes again with the pillow talk. What a hornbag.

Mil waddled over to the bed as Karen rolled onto her side, facing me, and began rubbing her daughter's back.

'It's okay, love, you'll be right.' she comforted.

'Fuck off, Mum.' came the retort.

Karen took another pull on the gas, gagged, and ripped off the mask in disgust.

'Here,' she said as she threw it in my general direction, 'Get rid of this, I'm gonna spew.'

I caught it before it hit the ground and proceeded to place the mask over my face, sucking back huge lungsful of the glorious nitrous oxide. I wasn't going to let this opportunity pass me by.

Mother and daughter both stared at me as I got stoned, mouths gaping like fish out of water.

'Waste not, want not.' I giggled as the drug started taking hold.

'Typical.' Mil said as Karen rolled her eyes to the heavens.

Not happy with the amount of oxygen seeping through the mask and diluting my hit I ripped it from the feeding tube, which I took into my gob and sucked like my life depended on it. That did the trick.

'Hahahahaha!! This gas is good fucking shit!'

(Five stars. Highly recommended.)

Not being one to pass up on a free high, Mil reached out her hand, 'Can I please have some M'Lord?' she asked.

'Typical.' I responded before sucking in another lungful.

My mother-in-law's face, dropped. I burst into fits of laughter. Karen, who we had completely forgotten about, moaned as another contraction took hold of her exhausted form.

'Just messing with you Mil, here you go.'

I handed her the tube and grabbed the camera, ready to start filming again. Mil wheezed as the gas filled her emphysemic lungs. Then she started giggling which set me off again and before long we were both in hysterics as we fed off each-other's amusement.

'Good to see you're both having such a good time!' Karen

scolded.

This just set us off even more, which did wonders for her mood.

Fortunately for Mil and I, the effects of nitrous oxide don't last long so we were back to our normal selves before we knew it. In the interests of self-preservation, we both chose not to indulge in any more gas until after Mugwomp had entered the world. Besides, I needed to be on the ball for the sake of my film, which I had decided to call "The Violation of Karen." Lucky we chose to stop when we did, as our midwife came back in to check how things were progressing. I'm fairly certain she would not have looked kindly on us exploiting the hospital's drug supplies for our own benefit.

About half an hour had passed since Karen had been induced.

'How you doing, love? Did you want anything for the pain?' the midwife asked.

'I'm fine thanks, but what are you offering?' I replied.

'She's talking to me, you fucking idiot!' shrieked the beast on the bed, then calmly she added, 'Look, I've been better but I think I can hack it.'

Karen was a machine and my admiration for her was only increasing as time went by. The verbal abuse was just gravy.

The two of them started talking about duration and frequency of contractions. I nearly died of boredom so I took this opportunity to make myself scarce and ducked out for a quick cigarette. I had smoked about half of it when I spotted Longshanks making his way over to me from the hospital entrance, waving his arms like a spastic octopus. Let me tell you a little about Karen's dad.

As his name suggests, the man was very tall and so thin

he could hide behind a strand of spaghetti. When he stretched his arms above his head passenger jets had to adjust their flight paths to avoid colliding with his hands. He is also a man with a similar temperament to my own and was not prone to panic. Seeing him in such a state was cause for concern. I stubbed out my smoke and ran towards him.

'What's up, Longshanks, is it time?' I called out to him.

'Nah, mate, but you better get back there.' he answered as we met up.

I gave him a quick once over. Longshanks had the look of a man that had been to Hell and back. I felt a knot forming in the pit of my stomach.

'Why? Is there a problem?'

'What? No, nothing like that, M'Lord. God, no. But please, come back. Karen will tear strips off me if you don't. Fuck me, she's an angry soul isn't she!'

'Got that right, old man. What did she say?'

'Oh, mate, I don't think you really want to know.'

'Nah, probably not, but hit me anyway.'

I braced myself for what was coming. Karen's tongue lashings retained their venom, even when delivered by a third party.

'OK,' he began, 'here it goes. And I quote, "You tell that stupid sonofabitch to get his fucking ass back to this goddamn room now or I'm gonna butt-fuck him with a cheese grater!" Sorry, M'Lord, her words not mine.'

Karen really needed to work on her anger issues.

A gaggle of nuns had overheard our exchange and the younger ones were crossing themselves like it was the end of days while the oldest one chastised them for their prudishness.

'Sorry, Sisters, that wasn't for your ears.' I apologised as

Longshanks and I made our way back into the hospital.

'Don't worry yourself, my son,' the elder penguin replied, 'your wife, she is with child, yes?'

'That she is, Sister.'

She turned to her initiates and pointed at me.

'That, my girls, is why we became Brides of Christ. When a woman opens herself to a man, she opens herself to the Great Enemy.'

In unison the group of younger nuns pulled rosaries from the folds of their habits and kissed the symbol of their Lord in an attempt to ward off evil (little did they know they were already in its presence). The Sister Superior continued her lesson as Longshanks and I stopped in our tracks, both curious to see where this was heading.

'Once her husband's seed fills her belly and begets a spawn of Satan, a fragment of the Fallen Angel possesses the mother. This can cause outbursts like the one we heard relayed to this poor son of Adam. Only when the child is born is the link to the Abyss severed and the mother's humours will finally return to normal. Better to fill ourselves with the Lord than the sauce of mankind my sisters.'

'Amen.' came the reply from the group.

Longshanks and I looked at each other and nodded in agreement.

'Makes perfect sense to me.' I said as we made our way to the elevator.

We returned to the labour ward as fast as possible and Karen's dad took a seat in the waiting room while I grabbed a bucket of ice chips as a peace offering.

'Goodluck, M'Lord.' he called as I opened the door to our room.

Fortune was on my side. Karen was in the throes of another contraction so was too busy screaming in agony to chastise me. I quickly ran a face-washer under the cold tap, wrung it out and dabbed the moist towel on her sweaty brow as the pain passed. While her eyes were shooting daggers at me, she didn't have the energy to scold and surprisingly gave me a weak smile as I placed an ice chip in her mouth. I gently kissed her dry lips and swore that Mugwomp would pay for the anguish she was causing her mother.

After about an hour Karen had reached the limits of her endurance and was finally asking for pain relief. I looked over to Mil who, yet again, was adjusting her bust in the mirror.

'Hey, Tits McGee!' I called to her, 'Make yourself useful and go find a nurse.'

With a huff she jiggled her massive puppies one last time before stomping from the room.

As we waited, I took Karen's hand in my own. 'Babe, I'm so proud of you. You're harder than a wedding night dick.'

'Thanks, babe. I hope it's all worth it.'

Before I could respond Mil returned with our midwife in tow. She made her way over to Karen and took her vitals as well as those of Mugwomp.

'So, your Mum says you're ready for some pain relief, darl'. How about some Pethidine?'

She didn't have to ask Karen twice. 'Yes pleeeeease.'

'No worries. I'll be right back.' The midwife updated Karen's chart and went to grab the drugs.

Twenty minutes and multiple contractions later she returned.

'This should help.' the poor excuse for a nurse commented as she fed the drug into Karen's bloodstream. Before leaving she had a look between Karen's legs and stated matter-of-factly, 'Sorry to say, but it looks like you've still got a while to go yet.'

'I don't think so,' came my wife's retort, 'I can feel her head in my arse.'

'Trust me, Karen, I know what I'm talking about. Hopefully those drugs should kick in soon.'

I couldn't bite my tongue any longer. 'Are you fucking kidding me? A blind, drunken honey badger would have more of an idea than you do.'

Before the imbecile could respond there was an almighty roar and all heads turned to the bed.

'I THINK IT'S COMING!' Karen bellowed.

The verbal stoush between the midwife and myself was over before it began.

"Nurse Ratchett" ducked back to have another look at my wife's business end.

'Well, fuck me. There's a head.' she said.

As I had been filming sporadically for the last half hour or so, my camera was in hand so I joined the midwife at the foot of the bed. Not a moment too soon.

'AAAAAAAAAAAARRRGH! I HATE YOU! GET THIS FUCKING THING OUT OF ME!'

Karen raged like an exploding nuke.

Just like a top fuel dragster doing the quarter mile, Mugwomp was expelled from her home for the last nine months in a torrent of filth. And I had caught it all on film like a champ.

It was at about that time that the Pethidine hit Karen. She was finally in the happy place she deserved.

As I severed the umbilical cord, I got a close look at the

muck covered beast before me. The little monster had a huge shock of thick black hair that was coated in congealed blood. I had never seen a baby with that amount of hair in my life. Mugwomp looked like a psychotic Troll doll. Spawn of Satan, indeed.

The midwife took my second-born away, weighed her and then handed her to me.

'What am I meant to do with this?' I asked incredulously.

'Clean her up.' was the response as she headed for the door, never to be seen again.

It would seem the midwife was holding a grudge after all.

'You have got to be fucking kidding me! It's not even mine. No one in either of our families has black hair. This is bullshit!' I whined, much like Will Ferrell in the comedy classic "Step Brothers".

Karen may have been too wasted to take note of my comment, but her mother certainly heard it.

WHACK!

From out of nowhere there was a smack on the back of my head. Nothing hard, more of a, "that's enough of your bullshit, M'Lord". I turned, filth encrusted baby held at arm's length. The look in Mil's eye said it all. Begrudgingly I made my way over to the tub filled with warm water that had magically appeared in our room. Before I could ask the harridan where it had come from, she said, 'Wash all that crap off *your* little girl, I'm gonna get Longshanks so he can meet his granddaughter.'

And in a puff of smoke the witch vanished.

'And fuck you too, Mil.' I mumbled as I proceeded to clean up the newest addition to the Chook clan.

As the gunk washed off Mugwomp I started getting a

better look at her. Even through the prune-like expression the tell-tale signs of E.E.S. were present. There could be little doubt this was my progeny.

A quick side note. Washing half clotted blood out of hair is a freaking nightmare, made even more difficult by the fact that the head it is attached to has the structural integrity of a cracked egg. I still remember how long it took to get that shit out, all these years later. Anyway, back to the story.

From the time she was expelled, Muggy, as she would come to be known, had been serene. Other than a brief squawk as she came into the world she hadn't cried, merely sucked on her fist. As I washed her, our eyes met and I saw the strength there. Even at this age there were signs of the determined, headstrong woman she would become. Yes, this child was mine. I just had to do something about the horns.

Finally, she was clean and dried, so I took her over to Karen, who was still pleasantly buzzing from the Pethidine. She smiled and reached out for her daughter, kissed her on the forehead and placed her onto her teat, which Mugwomp latched onto like a starving leech.

I took Karen's free hand and kissed it.

'You did good, gorgeous lady.' I murmured.

'Thank you, M'Lord. So did you.' Karen looked down lovingly at our daughter before continuing, 'Isn't she beautiful?'

'God, no! She looks like a hairy fucking potato!'

Four stars. I was finally a part of a natural birth and all the emotions that went with it. Karen showed me reserves of strength even I didn't know she had. I even managed to get stoned, which is always a bonus. Most importantly I recorded the whole thing. "The Violation of Karen" was a hit at it's one and only viewing, but that is a tale for another time.

Boris' V.E.D. (Finally, an Heir!)

Fast forward four and a bit years and Karen was gripped by the urge that many women are cursed with. She wanted to add another child to our brood. Having already sired two offspring I was hesitant to bring another one into the world. I was in my mid-thirties at this stage and by my calculations I would be child free in another fifteen years, (whether Mugwomp liked it or not). If we had another kid now, I would be pushing sixty by the time I got my life back. That was far from satisfactory. However, Karen, like all of the fairer sex, can be very persuasive when she wants to be. She is also as devious as a succubus and waited until I was at my most vulnerable before going in for the kill.

The opportunity presented itself one night while we were enjoying a few bourbons. Mugwomp was asleep in her cave and we were sitting outside listening to some sweet metal tunes. The music was thumping and my head was buzzing nicely. Karen refilled our glasses, put them on the table and then sat in my lap, draping one arm around my neck. Alarm bells should have started ringing then, but Karen is one hot woman and I was a sucker for her attentions.

'So, M'Lord,' she purred, 'Does Mr. Chuckles want to come out to play?'

An hour later we were lying in bed, sharing a cigarette and enjoying the afterglow of a job well done. That's when she struck, like a great white shark smashing into a surfer.

'Hey, babe, I need to talk to you about something.' Karen said, seemingly out of the blue.

Again, I should have seen what was coming but like the

fuck-drunk idiot that I was, I blundered into her trap like a fat kid into a lolly shop.

'And what would that be, my love.' I responded, a rare smile crossing my lips.

It's amazing how much good sex can alleviate the symptoms of Eastern European Smile. Unfortunately, it also makes you vulnerable to the wiles of unscrupulous women.

'Look, M'Lord, I really, really, really want another kid.' she said as she ashed the ciggy and handed it to me.

I took a drag and exhaled. Realisation was slowly dawning on me. I had another drag on the smoke before handing it back to my conniving wife. There was no way I was going to get played.

'Yeah, I know that, darl', but if we had another baby now then it will be twenty years before they're all fucking gone. I'll be an old cunt by then.' I was sticking to my guns.

'No, you won't.' The standard response.

'Yes, I will. Look, I want to enjoy at least some of my life before I die. If I have a kid now, that's not gonna happen. Sorry, babe.'

This banter went back and forth for a little while before Karen stubbed out the cigarette and argued, 'Old? I thought you were a Slav! A Ukrainian one at that! Pffffft, I bet you even fake having E.E.S.'

Game, set and fucking match right there. Karen knew I took pride in my heritage and constantly teased her about her weak Anglo blood. She knew there was no way I could use age as an excuse after she brought the superiority of my Ukrainian genetics into question.

'Nghhhhhhh,' I ground my knuckles into my eyes in frustration, knowing I had lost. 'Okay, you win. Let's have another one.'

Karen looked like Mike Tyson just after he had bitten a piece of Evander Holyfield's ear off.

'Fuck yes!' she cried victoriously before she planted a kiss on my mouth, 'Who knows, M'Lord, this one could be a boy.'

'I hope so, someone needs to keep the Chook name going.' I had resigned myself to contracting the disease that is parenthood for a third time, 'I won't be going to any antenatal classes though.'

Sometimes it's the little victories that help get me through the shitshow of life.

Ten or so months later and we were back in hospital although this time it was just Karen and myself. Also, as fate would have it, I would finally be welcoming an heir into the world. My unholy master had gifted me a son.

Like his sister before him, Boris refused to leave the womb of his own accord and once again Karen had to be induced. Unlike last time however, the medical staff were competent and the procedure was performed flawlessly.

While Karen's pain tolerance was impressive during Mugwomp's expulsion, she took it to the next level this time round. She made it quite clear that Boris' delivery would be drug free. If she pulled this off, my wife's name would be etched into the annals of history as One Hard Bitch.

I had intended to film the sequel to "The Violation of Karen." Unfortunately, the main star was less than enthusiastic in reprising her role. As we were preparing to go to hospital, she saw me putting a video camera into the inner pocket of my jacket.

'M'Lord,' Karen began.

'What's up, my delicious meatball of love?' came my

response. I have a repertoire of pet names I can draw on as well.

'What did you put in your pocket?'

'This.' I took the camera out and showed her.

It was like I had poured an esky full of ice water into an industrial deep fryer.

'You're fucking joking, aren't you?' Karen started.

The connection to the infernal regions all pregnant women have, was manifesting once again as a heat haze started forming above my wife's head.

'What? Don't you want a record of the birth?' I asked.

'Mate, are you for real? After what happened last time? No way. No fucking camera.'

'Pfffft. You can't be serious. What about your fans?'

The paint on the ceiling above Karen's head started to blister from the heat she was giving off. When she screamed it was as if all the demons of Hell also gave voice to her rage.

'NO! FUCKING! CAMERA! UNDERSTAND!'

'LOL! Whatever, you can't kill art baby.'

This was not what she wanted to hear. The incoherent roar of a thousand damned souls exploded from Karen's throat. She reached her left hand towards me and then swiftly raised it heavenwards. I suddenly found myself pinned to our bedroom ceiling, the force of the impact smashing the air from my lungs and knocking the camera from my grasp. Her right hand formed a fist and the videocam exploded in mid-air like a grenade, plastic casing and electronics flying everywhere.

'You bitch!' I gasped as I tried to fill my starving lungs with oxygen.

'HAHAHAHAHAHAHAHAHAHAHAHAHAHAH
AHAHAHAHAHAHAHAHAHAHAHAHAHAHAH

AHAH,' a brief pause as Karen mockingly took a deep breath, 'FUCKINGHAHAHAHAHAHAHAHAHAHAHAHAHAH AHAHAHAHAHAHAHAHAHAHAHAHAHAHAHAH AHAHAHAHAHAHAHAHAHAHAHAHAHAHAHAH AHAHAHAHAHA!'

Drawing on my extensive knowledge of the occult, I grimaced against the pain and forced words of command from my lips.

'THE POWER OF CHRIST COMPELS YOU!'

There was a sound like a thunderclap and Karen buckled to her knees as I hit the floor with a thud. The forces of darkness had been banished for now. I stood, dusted myself off and helped her to her feet.

'Holy crap, babe, that was metal as fuck!' I exclaimed joyfully, adrenaline coursing through my system.

'Shit yeah, babe. That was awesome.' Karen had the glint in her eye of someone that had tasted the power of a god and wanted more. 'Look, no filming, okay?'

I spread my arms wide, indicating the scattered pieces of the obliterated camera.

'Not like I have much of a choice now, is there?' I laughed as I held my devil-woman in a passionate embrace.

'Watch it, M'Lord, you'll squeeze the little bastard out.' she grunted.

'Sorry, babe, you know how demonic possession gets me all excited.'

And that is why I never filmed the expulsion of Boris. True story, I swear. It is also why there is no proof of Karen enduring the agony of childbirth without the aid of modern pain relief. Boris' entry into the world was truly medieval.

While the lack of a sequel to my first masterpiece is a

tragedy for the motion picture world, not needing to film allowed me to devote all my attention to my wife. If she was going to go all in with this V.E.D. it was only right I stepped up and helped her in any way that I could. Whatever she asked for, I provided. Water, ice chips, back rubs, virgin sacrifice, it didn't matter. If Karen demanded it, I made sure she got it.

True to her word, my wife endured everything that Boris threw her way. Sure, she screamed and wailed, joining the cacophony of pain emanating from the other mothers bringing their own spawn into the world, but not once did she ask for anything to ease her suffering. Karen had gone full beast mode. She brushed off the agonies inflicted by our son like they were merely inconveniences and not the tissue tearing violence they were becoming. Like a brute from the dawn of time Karen grunted and pushed, forcing Boris from her distended belly and into the cold light of day.

I don't know if her birth canal had become looser as a result of giving birth to Mugwomp all those years ago, but the boy was being expelled in record time. From the moment Karen's contractions began, to the instant Boris' crown appeared between her thighs, no more than an hour had passed. While her ordeal was nearly over, my wife was exhausted.

'I can't push any more. I'm done.' she cried.

'Come on, Karen, I can see the head. One more push and it's all over.' instructed the midwife, who had somehow appeared betwixt my wife's legs.

'I can't do it.'

As I wiped my love's face with a damp cloth my mind raced as I tried to think how I could give her the impetus for that one last push. Then it came to me. As I put my lips to her ear I whispered, 'I bet Screech could do it.'

'Fuck you, M'Lord!' Karen bellowed and with the last of her energy she forced Boris from her ravaged glory hole.

'Great work, babe! You did it!' I congratulated her as I gently squeezed her hand. After my previous comment I was not risking a kiss.

The pride I felt for my wife was immense. While there was little doubt that the demonic possession she had experienced earlier had amplified her stamina significantly, I could not take anything away from Karen's sheer determination. She saw this natural, drug free delivery through to the end. Words could not describe the admiration I had for her. She was a goddess in my eyes.

These feelings obviously diminished swiftly over time, as the realities of having to raise another shit machine bred a certain level of resentment. I kid, I idolise that bitch.

After cutting the cord that attached him to his mother, I examined the wrinkled meat-sack that was my howling son. His likeness to a scrotum was uncanny and I could only hope his unsightly appearance would diminish over time.

Unlike his older sister, Boris was not born with a thick mop of hair and was also bereft of horns. He was also wailing like a banshee where Mugwomp was much more stoic when she came into the world. Boris was, and still is, nearly the opposite of my younger daughter in both appearance and demeanour. Perhaps he is the yin to her yang, the calm to her storm, the good to her evil.

My boy would grow into one of the most compassionate kids I've ever known. Of all my children, he is the one least likely to kill me in my sleep. Every family has its black sheep I suppose and Boris is most definitely ours, as unlike the rest of my brood, myself included, he is a truly good person.

While his happy, selfless nature has made him the apple of his mother's eye, I secretly hope he's just going through a phase and outgrows all this "niceness" once he hits puberty.

Three stars. Being my third child, the whole experience was a bit ho-hum to be honest. At least it was over in about an hour. Karen would argue that it was more like three but I'm pretty sure she was delirious from the pain and had a limited grasp on reality, let alone time.

Conclusion

Well, these were my experiences with regards to childbirth, or V.E.D., as I prefer to call it. Every person going through it, either as the mother-to-be or part of the support crew, will have a different story to tell, so there is not much I can impart in the way of advice. If you are expecting a child then all I can say is good luck, because it really is a shitshow like you wouldn't believe.

Do try the gas though, it helps pass the time and is a pleasant, if short-lived, high.

Chapter 6:
The Violation of Karen: Why There Can Be Only One

It would be negligent if I didn't explain why Karen was so opposed to filming the birth of our son. After all, the debut of my first movie was a resounding success. One would have thought that she would have been chomping at the bit to follow it up with a sequel, but, as the previous chapter revealed, this was not the case. The following recollection will show it wasn't that Karen didn't want a visual record of Boris' expulsion, she was scared as to what I would do with it.

Take note those of you wanting to video the birth of your child. This is what not to do with the footage.

Yet again, my memories of the time in question are hazy at best. You may recall that Mugwomp was born one day before I celebrated the thirtieth anniversary of my own V.E.D. You may also recall that my actual birthday was the day before she was forced out of my wife's insides, and I wisely played it safe and did not indulge in excessive partying. When the time came to unleash the beast I had been suppressing for two days, I celebrated like it was the Catalina Fucking Wine Mixer. As a result, certain details have been erased from my mind even now. Nevertheless, I will do my best to ensure the events recounted below are as accurate as everything else recorded in this manuscript.

When the premiere occurred is of no consequence, suffice it to say it was a day or two after Mugwomp had entered our lives. Karen was still in hospital so was unable to make the screening. Knowing what I know now, this was undoubtedly for the best. From memory, a cadre of around a dozen of my closest friends were at our house in various states of intoxication.

'Oi!' I exclaimed.

'What?' came the reply from those still capable of speech.

'So, I'm a dad again.'

A raucous cheer was raised by the unruly mob scattered around my living room floor. My closest friend, the Hermit (remember him), staggered to his feet and signaled for the group to be silent. No one paid him any heed, so in frustration he bellowed, 'SHUTTHEFUCKUPYACUNTS!'

Silence. The Hermit was normally a quiet soul, a man of few words. He was known to rev up when he had a belly full of piss however and it was good to see him cutting loose. My brother-in-arms hadn't been himself since the night Karen attacked me in my sleep. He grabbed a bottle of bourbon from the coffee table, stumbled over and refilled my glass before topping up his own.

'A toast! Fill your glasses and grab another beer!' he called out as he raised his glass. Once he was satisfied that everyone had a drink he continued, 'To Karen, M'Lord's greatest conquest!'

'To Karen!' we responded as we skolled in her honour.

'Fill 'em up, boys, I'm not done yet.' The Hermit made sure our glasses were ready to go before shouting, 'To Mugwomp, the hairiest baby I've ever fucking seen!'

'To Mugwomp!' came the chorus.

He draped an arm over my shoulder while raising his glass one more time, 'And to M'Lord, Happy Birthday ya cunt!'

'M'Lord!' the rest of the group roared as the Hermit planted a kiss on the top of my bald head.

Gauging the crowd, I sensed the time was right to show the lads the greatest film since "Conan the Barbarian".

'Cheers, brother,' I said to my friend as I slapped him on the cheek before addressing the group as a whole. 'Hey, you lot, I made a movie of Mugwomp's expulsion. Want to watch it?'

The reply was unintelligible but amounted to a resounding, 'Fuck yeah!'

I found the camera and plugged it into the television and got the show started.

When I filmed Mugwomp's delivery I was thorough. Every single aspect of the birth experience was caught on film in explicit detail. I mean everything. Unbeknownst to my wife, I was about to show the group of vagabonds and ne'er do wells I call my friends parts of her no one other than myself had seen for years. At the time I didn't see what the problem was and pressed play without a second thought.

An hour later and the credits were rolling. The look on everyone's face said it all. My comrades were so in awe of what they had just watched that they were rendered dumbstruck and were unable to properly express their appreciation. This was understandable as "The Violation of Karen" truly was a cinematic masterpiece. I remember thinking this must be how Spielberg felt when he received his Oscar for "Schindler's List".

I tapped the Hermit on the arm, 'So, what did you think?'

'Fuck me, that was intense, M'Lord. Has Karen seen it

yet?'

'Nah, bro, why?'

'Dude, we saw everything. She's gonna lose her shit.'

'No way, she'll be right. What makes you say that?'

'M'Lord, we saw EVERYTHING.' He gestured spasmodically at his loins.

'So what? It's not like it was porn. Trust me, Karen will be fine with it.'

'Yeah, I guess.'

The look on the Hermit's face suggested that in actual fact he did not think Karen would be fine with it at all. Not one bit. Seeds of doubt were taking root in my drink-addled mind as to my wife's response.

'It's all good. She'll be right.' I murmured, more to myself than anyone else.

The next morning, I returned to the hospital to bring Karen and Mugwomp home while the Hermit stayed at my place to clear away the detritus from a night of hard drinking. It was only right that my wife and child came back to a tidy house, so he offered to clean while I picked my two little darlings up. Fucking legend.

****

'Hey, babe.' I said as I opened the door to Karen's suite. She gave me a kiss as I scanned the room. 'Where's Mugwomp?'

My devil-spawn was noticeably absent.

'Morning, darl'. She's just getting cleaned up. So how did yesterday go?' Karen enquired as she finished packing her belongings into an overnight bag.

My mind was racing as I tried to think of the best way to

tell her that her lady-garden had been seen by a bunch of my friends.

'Yeah, it was good. Hey, listen, I did a thing.'

Karen immediately stopped what she was doing and turned to face me, her body language betrayed nothing as she knotted the belt on her dressing gown. I knew better.

'A… thing?' she enquired, almost casually.

'Yeah, a thing.' I responded. The verbal sparring had begun in earnest.

A deep intake of breath followed by an equally lengthy exhalation was the only sign my wife's mood could potentially take a turn for the worse. Yet again, I was on very thin ice.

'What sort of thing, M'Lord?' she continued, 'A good thing? A bad thing?'

'Oh, definitely a good thing the way I see it, Lovemuffin.'

'Now I'm curious. Do go on, I insist.' Karen sat on the bed, trying to appear nonchalant but failing terribly.

'You know how I filmed Mugwomp's birth?' I began.

As if on cue a nurse brought my daughter into the room, smelling like roses and swaddled so tightly she looked like a hairy joint. The nurse was about to hand Muggy to the wife but I tactfully interposed myself and took my child from her.

'Come to Daddy, you little fucker.'

I was safe now. Well, safer anyway. The chances of being assaulted had just dropped dramatically. I doubted even Karen would risk striking her own child. Just to be sure though I put as much distance as I could between her and myself. The tension in the air was palpable, so much so that our little Florence Nightingale asked if everything was all right.

'Of course, darl', thanks.' Karen laid on the charm while I silently mouthed "Help me" to my potential saviour.

Whether it was some secret fucking sisterhood pact or the bitch was just blinder than Stevie Wonder, it didn't matter. The nurse left us to our devices and my interrogation continued.

'So, where were we? That's right, you had done a thing. A good thing wasn't it, M'Lord?'

'Correctamundo.'

It was as quiet as a tomb as we stared each other down. She raised her eyebrows and shrugged. I did the same.

'Well?' my wife broke the silence.

'Well, what?' I asked as I gently rocked Mugwomp while she slurped on her fist.

'What good thing did you do?

'That's right, soz. Remember how I filmed Muggy's birth?'

'Yeah.'

'Well, as you know I had a few drinks with the boys yesterday. Anyway, I got to thinking how amazing my camera work was and how it would be a shame to not share it. I asked the lads if they wanted to watch it and they were keen as fuck. So we did.'

I'm pretty sure I whispered that last bit into the palm of my hand.

'You did what?'

'Are you deaf? I said, me and my mates watched you having this little one.' I held my daughter out in front of me.

Karen's face drained of colour as she processed what I had done.

'How much?' she asked.

'How much what?'

'How fucking much did they see?'

'What, the movie? All of it. Babe, it was epic! You gotta

watch it!' I tried to put a positive spin on it for her but Karen was having none of it.

'No fucking chance! So you're telling me your mates have all seen my vag?'

'After a fashion.'

Karen buried her face in her hands and asked, 'How many? The Hermit?'

I did not want to answer but I had a shield in Mugwomp and my wife was going to find out one way or another. Better from me so she was forewarned.

'Probably twelve or so, and yeah, the Hermit was one of 'em.'

She lifted her head and her expression was a mixture of horror and despair.

'M'Lord, how could you show them my bits? I'm never gonna be able to look anyone in the eye again. Thanks a fucking lot.'

And then the waterworks started.

Despite the risk to myself, I plonked my little girl in the cot and took a seat next to my distraught wife, gingerly putting my arm around her.

'Oh darlin', don't cry. It's all good. There was that much blood and shit that it didn't look anything like a vagina. For fuck's sake, there was a damn baby's head coming out of it. It looked nothing like the sexy little coochie I know and love. Besides, everyone was that fucking hammered they probably can't even remember watching it. Don't worry.' I gave her a reassuring squeeze.

She wiped her eyes and blew her nose on my flannelette shirt, took a deep breath and leaned into me.

'You're probably right. You dickhead. What made you

think showing your mates my privates, was a good idea? Promise me you'll never show that movie to anyone else.'

'Yeah, no worries, babe. There's no one else I want to show it to, anyway. And just so we're on the same page I wasn't showing my mates your vag, I was showing them the birth of our daughter.'

I don't think I could have said it better. Karen was satisfied that it wasn't the end of the world and pressed her lips against mine, ramming her tongue down my throat until I gagged. I told you she was a hornbag.

I forced her off of me.

'Control yourself woman. So you sure you don't want to watch it?'

'I don't think I do, M'Lord. I'd rather not know what everyone has seen.'

Karen still hasn't watched the birth of her first child. Her loss, I guess.

And that is why I wasn't allowed to film my son's V.E.D. It didn't matter that the cinematography of this flick was so on point it was like watching a David Attenborough nature documentary. Karen did not think I could be trusted and would make the mistake of showing her lady bits to the world again. In her eyes it was better to be safe than sorry. When I think about it, she's probably right. I do like to stir up a bit of trouble from time to time.

Conclusion

I'll keep this brief. If you have filmed, or intend to film, the birth of your child and you record footage of the mother's nether regions, take heed if you value your life. Do not, under any circumstances, show these images to anyone until your significant other has given her explicit approval. Anything else is asking for trouble.

Even if the mother is an exhibitionist, she will not want her puss in the public domain when it looks like it's been through a freaking meat grinder. Trust me, it's not a pretty sight when a baby's head pops out of that hole. I didn't want to go back there for months after Mugwomp was born.

For the record, to this day I still don't see what the issue was. It wasn't like I wanted to show my friends where Mr. Chuckles goes to sleep at night, I wanted to share my joy with my inner circle.

In the end though, it all comes down to not doing things that will intentionally upset your better half. As the saying goes, "Happy Wife, Happy Life".

(Note to self: still waiting on the happy life bit to kick in. Further research may be called for.)

Part 2:
Raising Kids, What a Drag

"A child is a curly, dimpled lunatic."
   Ralph Waldo Emerson

"Parenting Hack: There are no hacks. Everything is hard. These kids don't listen. This is your life now. Godspeed."
   rookiemoms.com

"I finally had that talk with my kids. I told them that animals in the wild eat their young so they better get their shit together."
   cheezburger.com

"I live in fear of the day my kid asks, 'Where are all my other drawings?'"
   yellowdandy.com

"I want! I want! I want! Can I? Can I? Can I?"
   Every child ever fucking born

Introduction:
The Beginning of the End

I want to make something perfectly clear. Raising kids is hard, unrewarding work. Probably the worst thing you will ever do in your life. Nevertheless, there are some reprobates that will swear it gets easier as your children get older.

These people are delusional. In my experience, the opposite is true. The older your children get the harder it becomes.

My three offspring range in age from pre-teen to mid-twenties so I am familiar with every stage of a child's development. I can confidently state that infants are the easiest to look after. I would have sacrificed my right testicle for it to have remained that simple.

For the first few months of your young one's existence all you are required to do is feed them, keep them clean and clothe them. That's it. Piece of cake. Granted, sleep is practically non-existent for a little while but trust me, as your little darling gets older, being tired will be the least of your concerns. The worst part is changing a dirty nappy, but you do this until the little git is toilet trained anyway, so the point is moot. At least a newborn can't fucking run away mid-change, or take its own nappy off and smear faeces all over your walls. At this age they are at your complete mercy. If you put them to bed, they will not escape. They will eat whatever you give them and wear whatever you dress them in with no arguments. If you are a first time parent, take my advice and make the most of this stage while it lasts because it goes to shit oh so quickly.

Unfortunately, my eldest, Helga, did not get the memo. For the first month of her life, she would not stop screaming. Day and night she would cry so hard I was surprised the police didn't pay us a visit. To make matters worse she became more hysterical whenever she suckled. While I suspected it was because Screech's milk tasted of ash, we still took Helga to a GP. The diagnosis: gas. According to this doctor, and I use the term loosely, we just needed to burp her more thoroughly. Another week of constant howling proved this to be utter bullshit. What a fucking moron. I could have gone to my grandmothers and they would have told me the same thing. At least they would have given me a urine-soaked cabbage leaf to wrap around Helga's belly as a treatment. This quack couldn't even do that.

Lack of sleep and my daughter's constant shrieking had turned me into a monster. Everything made me mad. E.E.S. had nothing to do with my facial expression at this time of my life, I was living in a state of constant fury. I was even yelling at my own shadow because it wouldn't leave me the fuck alone. Sadly, I was also at the point where I wanted to put Helga into a mailbox and send her back to the foul pit that spawned her. Instead, I spent a lot of time outside pulling the wings off of ladybirds to distract me from the howls of the damned coming from within the house. In desperation, Screech took her to another medical clinic. Tests were done and it was discovered that my little girl was lactose intolerant. How shit is that! The only thing a baby can ingest when it is born is milk and Helga was allergic to it. What sort of twisted joke was the universe playing? Fortunately, the doctor was able to advise us of a baby formula designed for weak children such as ours and the screaming finally stopped. At last things were at peace in the Chook house and Helga was finally the immobile little meat sack that she was meant to be.

Let me make it clear that our experiences with my firstborn in that initial month were an aberration and not the norm for the vast majority of new-borns. My other two children were a breeze to deal with in the first few months of their lives. Then they became ambulatory and things changed.

When babies start crawling, walking or even scooting across the ground on their ass like some demented leper, the task of parenting becomes more difficult by a factor of at least a thousand. The change isn't gradual either, it's instantaneous. One minute your kid can't do a goddamn thing and the next it's tearing around your house like a freaking bull in a china shop.

Suddenly everything you own is fair game for your little sweetheart. You can buy child proof locks for all your cupboards but it won't do any good. They can't wipe their own ass but they'll neutralise any security you have in place like Harry fucking Houdini. You will end up with crap everywhere. Anything precious will become a target of priority and will either end up in your toddler's mouth or disappear, never to be seen again. Putting things out of reach provides temporary respite but it doesn't take long before the little shit learns to climb like a Cirque du Soleil acrobat. Once that happens, all bets are off. You will collapse from exhaustion before they do and then they will run amok unopposed. Your home will never be clean again.

Wait though, it gets worse. So much worse.

Once your little one learns to talk, you will have truly reached the nadir of parenthood. They just don't shut up. Ever. And because they are mobile you can't fucking escape them. Even if you lock the bedroom door behind you, they will still stand on the other side spouting a constant stream of drivel until you are curled up in a corner, rocking backwards and forwards, tears streaming from your eyes as you silently scream. You will pray for death, either yours or that of the creature you spawned.

So enjoy your new-borns while you can because it will never be that good again.

While raising children is a universally tragic state of affairs it is also a very personal experience. Every parent suffers through their own unique nightmare so it would be irresponsible of me to try and create a one-size-fits-all set of instructions. Instead, my intentions for this section are to provide a historical account of the ordeals I endured while bringing up my own brood. Luckily, there was no shortage of events to draw from. In fact, the most difficult part of writing this book was deciding what stories to include and what to cull or keep for the next volume.

Rest assured that every effort has been made to ensure that the tales that follow are as accurate as those in the preceding pages, so grab your drink of choice, crank up some Burzum on your music maker and buckle up for the ride of your fucking lives.

Chapter 7:
Mugwomp's First Birthday Party

A child's first birthday party is a soul sapping exercise in futility. The guest of honour doesn't even know what the hell is going on for God's sake! No one enjoys going to them. The only reason anyone does attend these poor excuses for a celebration is for the free booze, of which there had better be plenty. I hate going to them so much I will go out of my way to find the loudest, most obnoxious toy as a gift, purely out of spite. No, there isn't any space in this book for such a tedious event.

Instead, this chapter recollects the first birthday celebration my youngest daughter had the pleasure of attending. It was in actual fact the commemoration of my own expulsion. Thirty years had passed since that fateful day and it was going to be suitably epic.

Incidentally, Mugwomp was only one day old.

To avoid confusion here is a timetable of how things transpired.

1) Thursday: Karen was deposited at the hospital in preparation for Mugwomp's forced delivery the next day. This was my actual date of birth.

2) Friday: Mugwomp is banished from the womb. The Antichrist is born.

3) Saturday: the day we celebrated my third decade on

this godforsaken rock. I was finally becoming a man.

4) Sunday: the first and only screening of "The Violation of Karen". I think this was when it happened. As already stated, my memories from those days are a bit of a blur.

This story obviously took place on the Saturday night.

Karen had been planning this event for months in the expectation that she would have given birth and would be home to enjoy the festivities. As you know this was not the case. Due to Mugwomp being overdue, both my wife and child were still in hospital but Karen was not going to let this deter her. She had gone nine months without a drink and being the lush that she is, there was no way my wife was going to miss the party she had painstakingly organised. As I've stated ad nauseam, Karen is a hard woman that likes to get wild. She was not prepared to let her desiccated insides get in the way of a good time.

'So, big night tonight, M'Lord.'

'You've got that right, babe. It's gonna be the shit! A pity you can't be there.'

It was late Saturday morning and I was at the hospital with the Beauty and the Beast. You can decide who is who for yourselves. My better half was feeding my daughter, who was guzzling down milk like a black hole devours galaxies. I don't remember where Karen's parents were but let's just say Mil was taking Longshanks to the airport for his flight back to Queensland. My mother, Maleficent, and stepfather, Napoleon, had visited earlier that day. They hung around for half an hour or so, had a nurse of their new granddaughter and made it perfectly clear that we were not to rely on them for babysitting services.

'You decided to have a baby,' Maleficent stated, her voice

like ice, 'you look after her. Don't expect us to babysit.'

My mother was never a fan of children, especially little ones. This extended to her own young. It wasn't that she didn't love us, because she did, it was just that Maleficent has a low tolerance for childish antics. Playing is something alien to her. We get along fine now that I'm supposedly an adult (as much as Karen would argue otherwise). I think that the main difference between us is that as much as they shit me, I like messing around with my sprogs, it's just other peoples' children I can't stand, whereas my mother can't handle any child that hasn't hit puberty.

'Of course not, Mum. Who'd think grandparents would want to look after their grandkids? That's ridiculous.' I replied.

My stepfather started to snigger but was swiftly shut down by a withering glare from his wife.

'Not funny, M'Lord. Come now, Napoleon, give the child back to her mother and let's go. There's bound to be a party at a McDonalds somewhere and I feel like bursting some balloons. You know how I love the taste of baby tears.'

'Yes, dear.' He handed Mugwomp back to Karen and off they went.

Strangely, Napoleon loves kids. He was always down for a bit of rough and tumble. Honestly, him and my mother are so different I'm amazed they've lasted as long as they have. I think their secret is that Maleficent gives the orders and Napoleon just does what he's fucking told, whereas my relationship with Karen is built on a solid foundation of mutual antagonism and lust.

Anyway, enough of the time warp, let's get back into it. Karen and I had just discussed how freaking amazing my bash was going to be and I'd lamented how she wasn't able to attend due to having only spat out a kid one day before.

By midday I was bored beyond measure and eager to get the festivities started. The problem was I couldn't just leave without good reason or Karen would have lost her shit. Like a sign from Satan himself the theme from "The Exorcist" began playing. It was my phone. I pulled it out of my pocket and saw my man, the Hermit, was on the line. A plan started to take shape as I answered the call.

'What's up, brother?' I asked.

'Not much mate, everything's done. Grog's on ice, Barbie gas bottle is full, tables and chairs are set up. We are ready to party my man! How's the new fam getting along?"

'Oh, Christ! That's fucked!' I shouted.

'What's fucked?' Karen and the Hermit asked in unison.

I put my free hand up and signalled for Karen to be quiet for a minute while I tried to continue my conversation with my unsuspecting saviour. Not my smartest move.

'What's fucked, M'Lord?' my wife repeated. The dangerous edge to her voice demanded my immediate attention.

'Hang on, mate.' I told the Hermit before directing my focus to my nursing wife, 'Babe, the gas bottle is empty. I need to go home and get it filled before tonight or there won't be any fucking food.'

'Can't the Hermit go fill the bottle and you pay him back later?'

It was obvious that this was going to be more of a challenge than first thought. I put the phone back up to my ear, 'Mate can you fill up the bottle and I'll sort you out when I see you?'

'What the fuck are you talking about? I said the bottle is

full.'

Once again, I turned to Karen, 'He can't. He's spent all his money on booze and drugs for tonight.'

Then, before she could respond I was back on the phone, 'No worries, fella, I'll get it sorted. See you soon.'

I hung up before the Hermit could even reply.

'Sorry, darlin', gotta go.'

I got up, went over to my wife and child, kissed Mugwomp on the top of her deformed head as Karen detached her from her breast and put her over her shoulder for burping. I went to plant a kiss on my wife's mouth but she turned her head away and I ended up tonguing her ear.

'Oh c'mon! You've planned this for months. We've got a shitload of meat for tonight so I need to get the gas sorted. With all the madness of the past few days I guess I forgot to check if it needed to be done. Fucking sorry all right.'

'You'll come back once you've sorted it though, won't you?' Karen pouted.

'Probably not, my love. By the time I've gone home, grabbed the bottle, gone to the servo, filled it and then gone home again it won't be worth coming back. I'll see you in the morning, OK?'

I tried for another kiss and again I was deflected.

'This is bullshit.' Karen moaned, 'Like you said, I've spent ages getting your party organised and I can't even be there. It's not fair!'

'Yeah, I know, but it's not my fault, is it? Blame the beast you've got over your shoulder. She should have been here a week or two ago.'

As if on cue Mugwomp belched and shat herself at the same time.

I laughed. Karen did not. Wisely I took my daughter and proceeded to change her nappy.

As has been my wont throughout this treatise, I feel I need to digress once more.

The first few times an infant defecates the substance expelled from their bowels is not of this earth. It is so unlike normal faecal matter it has its own name, Meconium. It is no coincidence that it sounds like the name of some supervillain because this shit is nasty. It looks like tar, and like tar, it sticks to fucking everything and is nearly impossible to clean up. Fortunately, it does not smell too bad because if it did many new-borns would end up in the garbage chute, mark my words.

Finally, I got my girl cleaned up, wrapped, and as she was nodding off to sleep, I put her in her cot. I checked the clock and saw that after all that messing around it was pushing one thirty in the arvo. How time flies when you're having fun. I went to give Karen a kiss one final time and it was reciprocated at last, our tongues duelling like a pair of cobras.

Eventually I forced her off of me and said, 'Sorry, darl', I've got to go. I'll see you tomorrow all right.'

Karen glanced over at our child, who was milk drunk and passed out cold.

'I'll walk you out, M'Lord.'

'Cool.'

As we made our way to the elevator, I stole a glance at my wife from the corner of my eye. I could tell she was plotting something. We stood there in silence while waiting for the lift to arrive.

PING!

Finally, the doors opened and we stepped inside. I pressed the button for the ground floor and salvation. Still not a word had passed between us. It wasn't long before we exited the elevator and made our way to the hospital's main entrance. As we reached the automatic double doors Karen suddenly stopped in her tracks.

'You know what,' she exclaimed, breaking the silence, 'Fuck it!'

'Fuck what?' I ask, genuinely curious as to what prompted her outburst. Taking her by the hand I led her over to a couple of chairs near the gift shop and sat down.

'Your party.'

'Huh?' I was confused, 'Fuck my party? No, fuck you, sweet cheeks.'

'No, M'Lord, you fool. That's not what I meant. I mean, fuck it, I'm gonna come for a little while.'

'Where?'

'Home. For your thirtieth. I'm gonna break out for the night.' She was grinning from ear to ear.

'Oh.' was all I could muster.

'What do you mean, "Oh"?' Karen's smile was slowly transforming into a much more frightening expression.

'I meant oh great. That's a great idea.' I lied. I was actually looking forward to being family free one last time before the ball breakers came home for good. 'What are you going to do with Mugwomp?'

'She can come as well.'

Fucking great. Things were getting better and better.

'Really? Are you sure that's smart? She's only just been born.'

'Yeah, of course. We'll only come home for a couple of hours.'

'Okay. So you gonna come with me now?'

'What? God no. I'm gonna let the nurses watch Muggy while I get some Z's. I'll try and come up around seven.'

The only thing Karen enjoys more than drinking is sleeping. I'm pretty sure her spirit animal is an alcoholic sloth. Anyway, things were looking a whole lot better than they were a few moments ago. I was still gonna get a bunch of time partying with the boys after all.

'Yeah, sweet. You know I won't be in any state to pick you up though right.' By seven o'clock I expected my blood to be half bourbon, 'How will you get home?'

'I'll ask Mum to come get us.'

And, in an instant, things went to shit again.

'Are you sure? Will you all fit on her broom?'

'Be nice, M'Lord.'

'Yeah, whatever. Look I'm gonna go now. I'll see you tonight.' I gave Karen one final kiss goodbye and headed for the exit. 'Fly safe now.'

'I said be nice.' she called after me as I skipped out the doors, cackling like Broom-Hilda.

Half an hour later and I was cracking the seal on my first bottle of Wild Turkey. I poured the Hermit and myself two generous measures before adding Coke and ice. We clinked glasses and savoured the first of many mouthfuls of the amber-coloured firewater. It was early afternoon and the first guests were not expected to start arriving for a couple of hours. Plenty of time to relax on a couple of deckchairs, soak up some rays and shoot the breeze with my long time compadre. The Hermit swallowed another mouthful and sighed appreciatively.

'This is the shit, hey M'Lord?'

'Not wrong there, mi amigo.'

Things couldn't get much better. Great drink, great

weather and great company. I couldn't ask for more. And then the Hermit handed me a bong of sweet Mary-Jane. The final piece of the puzzle was complete.

'So how are mother and child?'

I coughed mid toke, 'Way to kill the mood, bro.' I finished the bong before continuing, 'Wife and child are doing fine. In fact, they'll be making an appearance tonight.'

I tapped out the cone piece, repacked it with nature's goodness and handed the hookah back. The Hermit lit up, one shot the lot and exhaled a dense cloud of smoke.

'Really, is that wise?' he asked.

'That's what I thought but Karen reckons it'll be all good. They'll only stay for a couple of hours anyway.'

'Ah cool. So how they getting here?'

'Mil's gonna bring em.'

'Will they all fit on her broom?'

Whiskey and coke exploded from my nose as I burst into laughter.

'That's exactly what I said to Karen.'

We clinked glasses once again, emptied the contents into our gullets and poured ourselves another.

'Hey, M'Lord, what was the deal with that phone call?'

I looked at the Hermit vaguely for a minute before the correct group of synapses fired up in my stoned brain and I remembered the conversation from only a few hours ago.

I sniggered, 'Look, don't worry about it, brother. That does remind me though, do me a favour?'

'Anytime.'

'If Karen asks you what I did this arvo tell her I had to fill the gas bottle up.'

A lightbulb appeared above the Hermit's head as he

worked it out for himself.

'Yeah, no worries.' he replied, matching my smirk with one of his own.

'Another thing,' I continued, 'if she asks why you couldn't do it, tell her that you didn't have any money 'cos you spent it all on booze and drugs.'

'I wouldn't be lying about that, bruv. Never fear, your secret is safe with me.'

Over the next few hours, people started arriving. In dribs and drabs at first but then a steady stream formed. Among the more notable guests to arrive were Maleficent and Napoleon. The look on my mother's face suggested that her hunt had been a successful one.

'Hey, Ma, you look like you had a fun afternoon.'

'Is it that obvious? Oh, M'Lord, we found a third birthday party for a pair of twins. The look of fear on the little bastards' faces when the balloons went Bang! It was priceless. Here, have a look, Napoleon filmed it.'

'Nah I'm good, maybe later.' I turned my attention to my stepfather and shook his hand, 'How do you put up with her, Napoleon?'

'She owns my soul, M'Lord.'

Knowing Maleficent as only a son could, this was probably true in the literal sense.

The night proceeded like a feast in the halls of Valhalla. Mounds of greasy barbecue meat were consumed and copious amounts of alcohol was drunk. I found a pair of clocks on the wall, well they were a pair until I closed one eye, at which point they merged into one. It was close to eight thirty. Maybe Karen and Mugwomp hadn't been given a pass out. Just as I was about to call the hospital a pair of headlights pulled up in my driveway. The country music blaring from the cab could only belong to one person. Mil had arrived with my wife and child. Curiously, I was legitimately happy that they had made it and I coasted down to the car as only a half-pissed Slav could. I managed to open the passenger side door on the second attempt and held out my hand to help Karen from her seat, swaying ever so slightly as I did.

'I didn't think you were going to make it.' I said as Karen stepped out and we embraced. 'What happened?'

After kissing me in the traditional manner she replied, 'Yeah, we had some issues. They weren't gonna let me go.'

The fools must have had a death wish.

'Oh no. So what did you do?'

'What do you think I did, M'Lord, I asked to speak to the manager.'

We both exploded into laughter. A minute or so passed before we were composed enough for Karen to continue.

'I just explained the situation, promised I'd be back by ten thirty and she was sweet with it. So here I am.'

In all likelihood, I had just been given a condensed, sugar-coated version of events. I expect that the reality of what transpired was more akin to Godzilla rampaging through Tokyo than a civilised discussion. There would have been casualties.

'So how many did you make cry?' I asked.

'Only four, including the nurse manager.' Mil interrupted as she came round from the driver's side of the car with my daughter and a bag full of nappies in tow. 'Hello, birthday boy, here's your present.'

She planted a lipstick smeared kiss on my cheek and handed me my spawn. I looked down at Mugwomp and found her staring back at me, her pitch-black eyes drilling deep into my soul. I extended the index and little fingers of my left hand into the Horns of the Beast and placed them over her eyes.

'Not tonight, Satan.' I whispered and the attempted possession ceased immediately.

'G'day, Mil, thanks for bringing them home. You hanging around?'

'Of course. It looks like it's going off.'

'It sure does. Having fun, M'Lord?' Karen asked.

'Fuck yeah, babe. Go and enjoy yourself. You only have a couple of hours so get stuck in.'

She turned and took a couple of steps toward the party before I called out, 'Hey! Karen!'

My wife stopped and turned back, 'What?'

'I'm glad you're here.'

She grinned, blowing me a kiss before making a mad dash to the eskies, her urge to consume alcohol overcoming any thoughts of decorum.

'Hey, M'Lord?'

I turned back to my mother-in-law, 'What's up?'

'Is your mum and Napoleon here?'

'Yeah. They're inside somewhere. Go find her, you could probably swap some spells.'

'Your witch jokes are getting old son.' Mil replied menacingly as she hung the nappy bag off my shoulder. Then she clicked her fingers and disappeared in her customary puff of smoke.

I lifted Mugwomp up so her nose touched mine.

'Not as old as her though, hey, my little darlin'.'

Within minutes of rejoining the party my daughter was taken from my arms and began making the rounds. I expected her to start crying as she was passed from one drunken embrace to the next but she took it all in her stride. Even from her earliest days Mugwomp clearly thrived on being the centre of attention.

Relieved of my burden I dumped the nappy bag in my bedroom and refilled my drink before rejoining the festivities. My memories from here on in are pretty vague if truth be told. One thing that stood out was Karen downing a yard glass filled with sparkling wine faster than Usain Bolt could run the one hundred metres. It had been nearly a year between drinks for the old girl and she was making up for lost time. And why not, she sure has hell deserved it after everything she had been through over the past few days.

The time eventually came for my wife and child to return to the hospital and not a moment too soon by all accounts. Karen was one drink shy of re-enacting the bar dancing scene from "Coyote Ugly" and Mugwomp had probably witnessed more degenerate behaviour in those few hours than most children will experience in years. The effects of this early exposure to drunken depravity are carried with her to this day as Mugwomp has always had a penchant for partying harder than most of her friends. She was truly blessed by the Gods of Metal that night.

When it comes to leaving a party, normal people say their goodbyes and call a cab or are taken home by the unlucky sod that was nominated as designated driver. These guys are unsung heroes, as hanging around a group of drunks while sober is one of the most infuriating things to ever have to deal with. No one ever says, "Went to a party on the weekend. I was designated driver. It was amazing!" do they? No. Always thank your DD, they put up with your fucked up asses all night and still make sure you get home safe and sound. Well done, you bloody legends!

That's how normal people leave. You have probably determined that my wife and I, and by extension our friends, are far from what could be considered normal. Just as Karen was about to stagger out the door some fool blurted out, 'Let's make a tunnel for bubs and mum to walk through.'

I do not know who it was but if you are reading this take note. You are a fucking idiot. How are we even friends?

For the next half hour, a gaggle of drunk women tried to organise a herd of even drunker men into a line so they could stand opposite each other with arms raised, hands linked in the middle. Like a shaft of staggering, stinking flesh fifteen metres long it went from the front door of our house to the passenger side of Mil's car. It took so long for this thing to form Karen was able to duck away for a quick spew and a coffee and had even started to sober up enough to realise something was taking shape. Christ, it took so long I had stopped seeing double and my speech was no longer slurred.

'What the fuck is going on?' my wife asked me, 'And where is Muggy?'

I performed a quick search, snatched my daughter from some random and handed her back to her mother.

'Some clown decided to form a tunnel for you two to go down.'

'Oh, how sweet.'

'Sweet? Are you serious? Can't you see what they've gone and done?'

'Yeah, like you said. Our friends have made a tunnel for me and your daughter to travel down. That's so cute.'

It seemed that my wife needed to be enlightened.

'That's right. And what is the tunnel made of, babe?'

After a few seconds thought Karen replied, 'People.'

'Good work. Now what are people made of?'

Another brief silence followed by, 'Meat. People are made of meat.'

Karen looked so pleased with herself as she kissed our daughter.

'Correct. Can you tell me what other sort of tunnel is made of meat?'

Her brow creased as her brain ticked over. Suddenly her eyes went wide with shock.

'Oh God. No. Oh, fuck me. They've made a birth canal.'

'You got it in one my love. Our friends have gone and made a big, fuck off birth canal for you and Muggy to walk down.'

'On the bright side, M'Lord, at least it's not full of blood and shit like mine was.'

'Yeah, true. Until someone chucks up.' I countered.

That was when the chorus started. First one voice, then another and within seconds the whole human meat tube was chanting, 'Karen! Muggy! Karen! Muggy!'

It was like a rabid crowd baying for blood as a prize fighter made his way to the ring. Except it fucking wasn't.

'C'mon, love,' Mil called over the ruckus, 'Let's go. I wanna go home to bed.'

I crushed Karen's lips against my own before planting a much gentler kiss on my little potato's cheek.

'Go on, babe, you best make a move. It'll be the witching hour soon.'

She gave my hand a squeeze and made her way through the heaving mass of inebriated humanity, the child of the devil clutched to her breast. Luckily for her (and all of our friends) everyone kept the contents of their stomach where it should be and Karen and Mugwomp were reborn at the end of the tunnel no worse for wear. A raucous cheer was raised as I buckled my daughter into her capsule and wished my wife farewell.

'I'll see you in the morning.' was the last thing I heard from Karen as my mother-in-law pulled out of the driveway.

'What? Morning? Fucking c'mon!' I called out as the car disappeared around the corner, "Jolene" blasting from the speakers.

Conclusion

And that was Mugwomp's first birthday party. While she was too young to remember anything from that night there is little doubt it prepared her for life in the house of Chook on a subconscious level. I also believe the love for wild partying was imprinted on her psyche from that point on and it is at least partly to blame for the hell this kid has raised all her life. I sometimes wonder if mother and daughter never came that night, whether Muggy would still be the out-of-control hellion that she has become. Then I only need to look at the family lineage she has been born into and realise the apple doesn't fall far from the tree.

Karen and I had no hope, we were damned from the start.

Chapter 8:
Scaring is Caring

I love to scare the shit out of Karen and the kids. Whether it's a simple jump scare or something more elaborate, I get enormous pleasure from the screams and looks of terror my mischief elicits from my wife and children. It never gets old. The family would beg to differ but I don't really care. Sometimes you just have to do what makes you happy and screw what anyone else thinks. Especially when you have to put up with as much crap as I deal with on a daily basis.

This kick I get from frightening my loved ones stems from my earliest childhood. I would have been five or six years of age. Old enough to have started school at any rate. As was common practice in those days, when school holidays arrived, parents would pack their kids off to stay with their grandparents. Mine were no different. Alternate holidays saw my brother and I staying with either my mother's parents, Baba and Did Goodtimes; or my father's creators, Baba and Did Chook. The events that I will describe took place at the home of the latter couple.

If you remember, Baba and Did Chook played pivotal roles in convincing both Screech and Karen that buying a new cot rather than using the old ancestral one I had refurbished would bring doom upon their children. You may also recall my grandmother invoking a being by the name of Baba Yaga when she gave her masterful performance that brought Karen to tears over the fate of Baba Chook's imaginary niece.

For those of you unfamiliar with Slavic folklore, Baba Yaga is an enigmatic old witch who lives in a hut that walks around on chicken legs. Crazy shit I know, but this sort of thing is par for the course when it comes to Eastern European mythology. In the tales told about her, Baba Yaga is neither good or evil and is just as likely to help as she is to hinder.

Not in my world. As far as five-year-old me was concerned she was the evillest, fucking bitch imaginable, thanks to my grandparents' twisted sense of humour.

Back when I was a kid the foreshore at Glenelg was a sideshow alley filled with rides and carnie games designed to part parents from their money. The crowning glory was a massive brown fibreglass turd from which waterslide tunnels emerged at various points, the squeals of happy children echoing from within. The name of this iconic sculpture? Magic Mountain. This monument to shit and good times, along with Alladin's Cave, an arcade of legendary status, were the centre of a thriving beachfront amusement park of sorts. Sadly, the whole lot was demolished in the late 1990's and early 2000's to make way for a marina and apartments that would serve as a new stronghold for Adelaide's elite. Nevertheless, I have so many great memories of Glenelg beach before it was defiled. So many, except for one.

The day that Baba Yaga came home.

I have no recollection which of the elder Chooks had won it, nor on which game of skill they had claimed their prize from. All I remember was Did Chook waving the most horrifying head I had ever seen in front of my face while booming in his Russian Mafia boss accent, 'Look M'Lord, is

Baba Yaga. Watch out, she be eating you!'

Fuck him. Even now, some forty plus years later I can still see that head as clear as if it was yesterday. It was the size of a small grapefruit with skin as white as corpse paint, long straggly hair as orange as, well, an orange and a long, hooked nose festooned with warts. The eyes were the worst though. Set beneath a craggy brow, two red orbs with pupils slit like a snake's, stared out at me with a malicious hunger. Logical, adult me knows this is impossible. A plastic head feels no hate and is incapable of inflicting harm. However, little, innocent me knew that motherfucking witch wanted to swallow me whole. Nothing before or since has scared me as much as that damn head did.

Baba and Did Chook knew it as well and they had every intention of milking it for all it was worth. From that day on until I was old enough to take matters into my own hands, they would pull Baba Yaga's disembodied head out and chase me round the house and yard with it, cackling and sniggering like the demented fuckwits they had become.

'M'Lord, come give Baba Yaga a kiss.' they would call out as they chased me down the hallway.

'WAAAAAAAAAAAAAGH!' I would scream hysterically as I ran as fast as my useless little legs would carry me. My incoherent wailing could be loosely translated as, 'You and that head can fuck right off back to the gulag that spawned you!'

I remember wishing they would choke on their false teeth as they guffawed in uncontrolled fits of laughter while I cried like a nancy-boy. Life in the old U.S.S.R must have truly been something else if this was how people from the old country got their shits and giggles.

After a year or so I became inured to their tender ministrations. The head of Baba Yaga, while still frightening, was no longer a source of pants-wetting terror for me. Instead, I began following in my elders' footsteps and started tormenting my younger brother, Goldenboy, in the same way, much to Baba and Did Chook's amusement. The pair of them would sit on the back porch shedding tears of joy as I chased him around the yard with the plastic head held above my head.

'HAHAHAHAHAHA! Come to Baba Yaga!' I would scream in that annoying, high pitched voice all little kids have as I mercilessly pursued my hysterical younger sibling.

Not satisfied with such simplistic methods of torture I turned my childish intellect towards more satisfying methods of inducing fear in Goldenboy. Instead of chasing him, I started leaving the witch's head outside the toilet door. If anything, my little brother was even more traumatised by Baba Yaga than I was and he would rather soil himself than go anywhere near that damned witch.

My grandparents finally ceased in their efforts to mentally scar me. When I started scaring the crap out of my younger brother it was as if I had passed a rite of passage and I had become a fully-fledged Chook.

This love of the scare gag has stuck with me ever since, much to the chagrin of those that call me Father and Husband. The sheer number of scares I have inflicted on my loved ones is staggering. There are however standout moments that make me laugh even now. Allow me to elaborate.

The Time Karen Forgot How to Scream

I have managed to pull this feat off, a fair few times, in more than twenty years of indentured servitude to my beloved wife but, like murder, it's the first time that you never forget. What I'm talking about is when someone is so frightened that they go through all the motions of producing an ear-splitting scream of terror, but are unable to make any sound.

The first time this happened was in the early years of my relationship with Karen, back when things were still fun. We were in the lounge room watching some shite on the television when she decided to have a shower. As soon as she had left the room a familiar voice piped up in my head.

'Hey, M'Lord.'

'Hey, Evil Me, wassup?'

'Not much. Wanna do something fun?'

'Sure. What did you have in mind?'

'How about a bit of the old faithful?'

'Hmmmmm,' I thought, 'Scare Karen? I dunno, she lost her shit last time we got her in the shower remember? Besides, I think she keeps a knife in there now.'

'Don't be a fucking pussy, M'Lord.' Evil Me didn't hold back, 'You know we love it. Besides, I wasn't thinking of a shower scare, they're getting a bit old anyway.'

'Well, now you've got my interest. Do go on.'

'What if we went and stood in the wardrobe behind Karen's clothes and got her as she started getting dressed?'

'Could be dangerous. Let me think about it.' I communicated to my darker nature.

'Whatever. You gotta risk it for the biscuit. What happened, did she take your balls as well as your freedom?'

Evil Me could be a cruel bastard when he wanted to be. He was not averse to emasculating me into making poor life choices. To my credit I tried to ignore him.

'Tick tock, tick tock. C'mon, man, you know it'll be

hilarious.'

The peer pressure was too much to take and I buckled, 'Fuck it, I'm in.'

'That's my boy.' Evil Me hissed as he was subsumed back into my subconscious.

I made my way to our bedroom and stepped into the walk-in robe, secreting myself behind Karen's ample collection of dresses and waited, like a trapdoor spider ready to pounce on its unwary prey.

Like most women, Karen can spend a long time in the shower. After twenty minutes my interest started to wane and I was about to give up on my endeavours when I heard the water stop running and the shower screen slide open.

Not long now.

The bathroom door opened and I heard padded footsteps make their way down the hall and into the bedroom. Suddenly I found myself suppressing nervous laughter that threatened to give me away.

'Keep it together.' I thought to myself.

'Yeah, keep it together, M'Lord.' Evil Me warned before sinking back into the depths of my soul once again.

I heard a towel drop to the floor before a stream of light shone into the wardrobe as Karen slid the door open. Fortunately, the sheer quantity of clothes owned by my future wife ensured I was still safely hidden away. I held my breath as I waited for the perfect moment to strike so as to achieve the maximum scare factor possible. In the end though, this decision was taken out of my hands as Karen parted the hanging clothes in her search for something to wear.

I may have neglected to mention that I had put on an ice hockey mask splattered with vast quantities of fake blood.

As she slid the dresses aside, poor Karen was greeted by the greatest mass murderer ever created for the silver screen.

'Ki, Ki, Ki, Ma, Ma, Ma.' My Jason Voorhees alter ego whispered as all the colour drained from my betrothed's face. She opened her mouth to scream but nothing came out and was shaking so hard all the jubbly bits I love were putting on a fine show. Karen tried to scream again, but to no avail. Her fear was so great it had not only stolen her voice, but had also rendered her immobile, like a kangaroo stunned by a car's headlights. This was the greatest scare I had ever executed. The only thing that could have topped it would be if it had happened on Friday the Thirteenth.

'Outstanding.' Evil Me commended, and rightly so, 'You better take off the mask before she dies of fright though.'

I stepped out of the wardrobe, slowly pulled the mask from my head and started chuckling.

'Oh my God. That was gold. You should see your face.' I remarked triumphantly.

Karen was still standing in stunned silence, arms at her side. She reminded me of a guard at Buckingham Palace and this amused me even more. I made my way over and embraced her from behind so as to limit any potential violence-based retribution.

'You okay, babe?' I asked as I wiped away a tear that ran down her left cheek, 'I have to say, you'd be fucking useless if we ever had a home invader.'

Slowly she stopped trembling, regained her wits and said softly in a shaking voice, 'You fuckhead.'

My work was done here.

Five stars. Well worth the effort. Will certainly be back for more.

Quick, We Have to Get Back Before Dark!

The inspiration for this scare was taken from the cult classic "The Evil Dead." The original that stars Bruce Campbell, not the remake (which is a great film in its own right by the way). There is one scene in this movie that stands out to anyone that has seen it. That's right, the bit featuring that icon of horror, the evil, rapey tree. It was the premise of a possessed tree that gave rise to the terror that was experienced by each of my offspring.

Like all people of note, I have always shared my life with a dog. Exercising these most excellent companions is to be expected and I made sure that the ones I have owned were walked on a daily basis. I enjoyed these moments of solitude, tromping about the neighbourhood with my four-legged friend. As well as helping me retain some semblance of a healthy lifestyle, these walks allowed me time to just think. Not about anything in particular, just whatever weird and wonderful things that pass through my mind at any given time. Then I had kids and like everything else associated with raising a family, walking the dog started to suck some major ass.

It was fine while my brats were motion compromised. I would just load them up in a pram and they would accompany me and my boy Rommel, a white and brindle pit bull cross, on our journeys. Even after they took their first steps, they would prefer to be pushed rather than walk of their own accord. I could still go at my own brisk pace. However, by the time they got to three or four years of age they wanted to walk by my side and that's when walking the dog went to shit. I know, it sounds so sweet in theory, a time for father and child to bond while getting a bit of fresh air and exercise. What a load of crap. The reality of the situation shatters said theory like a wrecking ball into a glass house.

The problem was, when my kids were small, they were so damn slow and had absolutely no stamina to speak of. I blame the Anglo-Saxon side of their ancestry. Pure Slavic children were hunting bears by the time they reached the age my children were at. Trips that used to only take half an hour became hour long journeys of frustration as they had to constantly stop and rest. And the whining was incessant.

'Can we go home now?'

'It's so faaaaaar.'

'My legs are tired.'

'Shut up for God's sake!', I would rage internally.

Most of the time I would end up slinging whichever child it was over my shoulder and walking home in disgust. I ended up shortening the distance we went to compensate for their feeble constitutions but they were still too slow for my liking and prone to bouts of verbal diarrhea, a common ailment experienced by children of all ages. I had to make these trips quicker before someone died.

One day a solution hit me in the face like a cinder block. I was waiting on a street corner for Helga to catch up yet again. The sun was setting and the afternoon was slowly turning to evening.

'Oh, fucking hurry up.' I remember thinking as I watched my firstborn stagger past a crooked gum tree. That's when the idea formed in the cesspool that passes for my mind.

'Hey, Helga, we have to hurry. We've got to get home before it gets dark.'

'Why Dad, I mean, M'Lord?'

Nice save. Helga was always sure to try and use my correct title.

'Because when it gets dark the spirits come out of the trees and attack people.'

I then proceeded to explain to Helga how during the day the evil tree demons are trapped inside their arboreal prisons but as night asserts its dark influence, they are free to terrorise the living. Now, little children are gullible and can be convinced of almost anything. It didn't matter that we had been walking at night many times before and had never been set upon by any malignant forces of darkness. From that point on, as far as Helga was concerned, every tree and shrub harboured an evil entity that meant her harm once the sun went down. They were as real to her as Santa, the Easter Bunny and the Tooth Fairy.

Henceforth little Helga tried her heart out to walk as fast as her stubby legs would carry her. Whenever she showed signs of slowing or complaining I would nervously glance at the darkening sky and then the trees, making sure that she saw me doing so.

'C'mon, darlin',' I would plead, 'We're running out of time.'

That's all it would take. She would glance at the sky, stop her whining and pick up the pace. I'm not going to lie, progress was still slow because little children have little legs and just can't take big steps, but at least we weren't being overtaken by snails any more.

The tale of the possessed trees was so effective in getting Helga to walk at a speed more conducive to my needs, I chose to use it on both Mugwomp and Boris when they started joining Rommel and myself on our daily strolls. As expected, it worked a charm, so much so, if I needed time alone, I would delay my walks until it was dark. There was no way my little ones would join me once full night held the land in it's dark embrace.

Of all my brood, Mugwomp was the one most affected by the demon trees. All these years later my other two can't even remember the story but recently Muggy and I were discussing what memories I was going to include in this book when she brought up this tale. She went on to blame it for her fear of the dark. Whatever, I think she just needs to drink a cup of cement and harden up.

Before all you do-gooders grab your pitchforks and hunt me down for some perceived trauma I have inflicted on my kids, have a look at yourselves. How many of you perpetuate the myths of that filthy trinity I briefly touched upon earlier: Santa, the Easter Bunny and the Tooth Fairy? That's what I thought. Likewise, how many of you have used the threat that these mythical beings will punish your spawn if they misbehave? Christ, in Europe, Santa has a demonic servant called Krampus whose only role is to kidnap and beat naughty children.

Every parent ever has relied on their kids believing that they will not get presents at Christmas if they act up. I know Karen and I had a direct line to Santa and every time our young would run amok, we would be on the phone letting the fat bastard know that the child in question was giving us grief and needed to be added to the naughty list.

Face it, as parents, we need to use every dirty trick we know to get our little beasts to behave in a manner appropriate for their continued existence in the world of the living. I regret nothing.

Aaaaah! A Spider!

While I have a deep-seated hostility towards humanity's ever-growing addiction to social media there are some damn fine pranks which can be trawled from its unwholesome depths. This is one of my favourites that I found on the Facebook. I love it so much I plan on using it on any grandchildren my offspring may produce.

All you need is a roll of toilet paper and a black felt tip pen. Unroll a good few metres of the paper, but be careful not to detach it from the main roll. Then draw a hairy, black spider on the outward facing side. You don't need to be Van Gogh, a black circle with eight legs will do but the more effort you put into your rendition of an arachnid the better chance you have of pulling off a ripper of a scare. Do not draw a web, that's a fucking stupid idea. Spiders don't build webs within sheaves of toilet paper. Once you're happy with your illustration, carefully roll the paper back up, making sure it doesn't look like it has been tampered with, and place it on the toilet roll holder. Then you just have to wait.

I prefer to draw my hairy, little horror inducer around half way through the roll so that it can take days before the spider is revealed. I've even been known to draw one on an as yet unused roll and put it back into the pack with its arse-wiping brethren. I have discovered this gag brings me the greatest joy when I have forgotten I have even set it up. The happy tingles you get when someone you love screams hysterically while emptying their bowels (literally) can only be exceeded when you suddenly remember why they're screaming in the first place. Remember, scaring is caring. And I care a lot.

My preferred victims for this prank are Karen and Boris,

partially due to their irrational fear of all things creepy crawly, but mainly because their wails of terror are so hilarious it maximises my return on investment. However, the nature of the gag makes it a crap shoot as to who you will catch out with it. Once I even scared myself.

There I was, having just purged myself of the grog bog from hell. I had just pulled a few sheets of paper off to wipe myself clean when I spotted a tiny, black, eight-legged freak sitting on the roll.

'Fuck me!' I cried out.

'What's wrong? Are you okay, M'Lord?' Karen called from down the hall.

I chuckled when I realised, I had just pranked myself. 'You twat.' I thought before replying, 'All good, babe. I just got some shit on my finger.'

There was no way in the seven hells I was going to give Karen the pleasure of knowing I had just fallen victim to my own joke.

'Yuck,' came the reply, 'That's disgusting.'

'Well, you asked.' I responded.

It's not in me to let a good trick go to waste so once I had cleaned myself up, I found a texta and locked myself back in the toilet so that I could redraw my take on a red-back spider, ready for the next unsuspecting member of my family.

Way back in the introduction to these hallowed pages I made it clear not to use this book as some form of parenting guide. By now you can see why, but out of anything contained herein, I can recommend using this scare. It's harmless and as long as you leave enough time between repeats it never fails to amuse. Just don't go overboard as it will lose its scare factor and you will just become a dick. Trust me, I know this for fact.

Don't save it just for the family either, anyone is fair game. I remember that I was using the Hermit's toilet once and chose to play this trick on him. A week later he came over for a few drinks with Karen and myself.

'Hey, M'Lord, you'll never guess what happened.'

'Well, do tell.' I said, oblivious as to where this conversation was going.

'You'll never believe it. I was having a crap last week and went to wipe my ass and some dirty bugger had drawn a huntsman spider on my toilet paper. I fucking shat myself. Again!'

That's when I remembered what I had done and started laughing hysterically as Karen kicked me under the table. I gave her a look that basically said "don't say a word", wiped the tears from my eyes and replied to the Hermit, 'Oh mate, that's gold. Whoever did that is a fucking legend. Do you know who it was?'

'Nope. But I have my suspicions.'

He stared at me for what felt like an age before lighting a cigarette. I made sure I was as unreadable as a rock.

'What? Bro, you can't think it was me, surely?'

'Who else could it be, M'Lord.' The Hermit looked at Karen, 'It was him, wasn't it?'

Try as she might, Karen couldn't (or wouldn't) keep a straight face and proceeded to throw me under the bus. E.E.S. doesn't mean shit when your other half is guffawing like a donkey.

Exasperated, I said to her, 'Thanks, babe, good to see you have my back, you fucking traitor.'

Turning to mi amigo I shrugged and said, 'So you got me. Sorry, not sorry.'

'All good, mate.' he chuckled, 'You got me a ripper. How did you come up with that?'

'How do you reckon, the Facebooks.'

'Of course. I think I'm gonna use it at work.'

'Noice. Let me know how it goes.'

'Will do, bruv.' he responded with a shit eating grin on his face.

So have some fun with this one. Change up your spiders. However, be careful not to use it on someone with a weak heart. Unless you stand to inherit something from their demise of course. Note that decision is on you though. I take no responsibility for your actions, you stone-cold bastard.

Conclusion

Being a husband and a father can be a right pain in the ass at times. Karen and the kids can sometimes shit me just by existing.

It's not their fault, but because of them, my dreams of becoming a guitar god in some evil fucking black metal band turned to dust when they became a part of my life. Shit, who am I trying to fool, of course it's their fault.

All that is left to me now is to eke out some small measure of happiness, any way that I can. One way, as described in this chapter, is to scare the ever living shit out of those closest to me. I make no apologies for that. We all do what we can to stay sane in this crazy world.

Chapter 9:
The Joy of Sharing Your Home With Beasts

Don't fool yourself. The children you have the misfortune of sharing your home with are as far removed from civilised humanity as Neanderthals, maybe even more so. Granted, some exhibit a thin veneer of cultured behaviour when out in public or visiting friends and family, but this is just an act, comparable to dressing a chimpanzee in a tuxedo. It might look cute, but it will still fling handfuls of shit and tear you limb-from-limb, given the opportunity. Your kids are no different.

As the saying goes, you can polish a turd but it is still a turd.

This criticism of our spawn is not aimed solely at the younger ones. From new-borns through to young adults that have yet to fly the coop, they are all the same. Beasts that keep on taking all that they can with minimal urge to contribute to the household in which they reside. Parasites, one and all.

Once a child moves out and experiences the full gamut of life in the real world, both the ups and the downs, they come to realise the sacrifices their parents had to make to keep the family unit operational. That's when they finally appreciate all that you have done for them and the whole relationship dynamic changes into something more tolerable. Until that happens though, they are just leeches and destroyers of hopes and dreams. I would call them all lazy cunts but Karen says that I shouldn't use the "c" word when describing our children so I won't. They are though, and so are yours.

While on the topic of lazy cunts I am unable to proceed until I broach the topic of children, if you can call them that, in their twenties and sometimes even their thirties that have never lived away from the family home. What the fuck is their problem? They need to be told to pack their shit and get the hell out.

We have a limited time on this planet and should be enjoying the second half of our lives without a care in the world, not cleaning up after our adult offspring. Birds are kicking their young out after a few weeks so I think twelve years is more than generous. I kid, but in all seriousness, by nineteen your child should have moved out at least once, even if only temporarily. The sooner that they learn what the real world is all about, the better. Knowing what it takes is the first step in being successful on whatever path they choose to follow. By the time they're twenty-five they should be gone for good. The only time they should visit from that point on is to drop off grandchildren or to wipe our arses when required.

So if you fit this category and are reading this, feet up on your parent's coffee table, put the damn book down immediately. No doubt it's your mother's copy anyway. Get on a device that links you to the internets, look up realestate.com or whatever it's called and find a place of your own to live. Rent or buy, it doesn't really matter. Your parents are sick to death of you. Honestly, they can't even bear to look at your face any more. Stop being a burden on them and finally go live your best life. Trust me, neither you or your elders will regret it.

That needed to be said.

Basically, living with your children is not much fun. It would be so much better if they lived in a communal home somewhere and were cared for by trained professionals. Similar to how the Spartans raised their own young.

As parents we could visit and take our mini-me's out on excursions or even take them home for sleepovers if the urge really took us. However primary care would fall to those that choose child rearing as a career path. Obviously, they would need to be trained to high standards and paid generously. After all, the future of humanity is in their hands.

Taken to extremes, these dormitories and educational facilities could also be used to sort the wheat from the chaff so to speak, again much like the Spartans did in times of yore. A form of population control if you will, where only the best humanity has to offer survives.

Unfortunately, short of tearing society down to its foundations this idea will never bear fruit. As a species we have developed a very unhealthy attachment to our young. It would take a well overdue reworking of the outdated idea of the family unit for my vision to become a reality and that is most unlikely. One can still dream though.

I have found it was simpler, both from a writing and reading perspective, if I sorted my tales so that stories of a similar nature were grouped together. It also allowed me to deal with my memories in a way that meant I did not have to revisit certain traumatic events more than once.

We will begin with the thankless task that is ensuring the appetites of our broods are satisfied.

"For God's Sake, Just Eat It!"

Initially my young ones would eat anything. Veggies, fruit and meat in all their tasty forms, it didn't matter, they loved it all. Then one day, out of the blue, everything changed. With the exception of Helga, feeding them became an onerous chore that could be likened to having teeth pulled. Every single one of them. Without anaesthetic.

I'm certain they became fussy eaters the moment they ate junk food for the first time. All those artificial flavours and the massive sugar hit was not like anything they had ever experienced before. For example, when Boris had his first sip of Coke, I watched his pupils dilate as if he had just snorted a line of speed. Then, as the caffeine kicked in, he started bouncing around the room like the ball in a pinball machine. He fucking loved it.

As far as their unsophisticated taste buds were concerned, processed food was the shit now. Everything they used to eat with relish was suddenly off the menu. Mealtimes turned the dining table into a warzone from which no one escaped unscathed.

Of all my children Helga was the most open to eating what was put in front of her. Her mother and I separated when she was around two, with custody of my daughter going to bitchface. It was at this time Screech decided to become a vegetarian and by default so did my firstborn. When Helga came to stay with Karen and myself there were always packets of fake meat sausages, patties and other protein substitutes stowed in her bag amongst her clothes and toys.

Initially, we humoured my ex, and cooked this pretend flesh alongside our own until curiosity got the better of me, and I had a bite of one of Helga's tofu burger patties. I wouldn't know, but I bet that's what eating diarrhetic hippo arse tastes like. I vowed from that point on my little girl was not going to eat that crap while she was at my abode. The next time she came to stay I took all of the pretend meat and gave it to the dog, knowing full well that he eats everything. No word of a lie, I once watched Rommel eat a gigantic shit Boris laid on the driveway so you would think he'd eat vego burgers, right? They do look the same after all. Not a chance. He had one sniff of what I had dumped into his bowl and then looked at me as if to say, 'What the actual fuck, bro. I guard your house and you try and feed me this garbage?'

The fact that my dog would sooner eat human waste than what vegetarians try to pass off as a protein alternative says a lot about how it tastes.

Disclaimer: I've since been told that if you add spices and other flavourings, meat substitutes can taste all right. Also, bear in mind that this was more than twenty years ago. By all accounts today's vegetarian fare has come on in leaps and bounds, but honestly, it will never compare to the taste of the real thing.

From then on Karen and I would just cook regular meat and tell Helga she was eating vego food. This went on for a couple of visits but one day, as she was wolfing down a juicy chop Helga asked, 'M'Lord, is this real meat?'

'No way, darl'. I know you're vegetarian.'

'You're lying.'

I cocked one eyebrow. 'What makes you say that, Helga?'

'Because it tastes good. Mummy's food is okay but it doesn't taste this good. And—' she paused, looking at the chop in her greasy hands.

'And what babe, go on.' I encouraged her.

She looked up at me, holding out her cutlet, 'Well, it's got a bone, M'Lord.'

I couldn't keep the charade up any longer. 'Yeah, it does kiddo, it's got a bone. You're eating lamb chops. Nice huh?'

'Yep. You won't tell Mummy I'm eating meat, will you?' Helga said as she gnawed on what was left of the rib in her hand.

'No way. It'll be our secret.'

Like I was going to tell Screech that I was feeding our daughter delicious animals. I would rather stab knitting needles into my ears than listen to her lecture me about the evils of the meat industry. My house, my rules as far as I was concerned, so the banshee could go jump in a lake of boiling lentil soup before I would let her tell me what to feed our girl while she was staying under my roof.

It was little wonder that she was so easy to feed when all she ate at her mother's house was as tasty as eating cardboard. Screech had unintentionally made feeding Helga a breeze.

The same could not be said for Mugwomp. She could sit at the table for hours gagging on boiled carrot and sauce sandwiches because it was the only way she could get the carrots down. And before you get all judgmental, no, that wasn't the only thing that we fed her for dinner. We aren't that cruel. Muggy would always leave her carrot to the very end of her meal and burying the taste of the vegetable in bread was her way of eating it.

Getting this kid to eat anything other than chicken nuggets, fish fingers and chips was near impossible so I would resort to subterfuge to get her to eat vegetables.

For example, I would squash peas and carefully slice open nuggets or whatever other garbage she was having for dinner and hide the little green buggers inside. This worked for a little while but Mugwomp isn't stupid and caught on to what I was doing. Mealtime became a game where she would search for vegetables hidden amongst the rest of her food.

In the end the only veggies I could get her to eat were broccoli and cauliflower. These had to be boiled until they were limp and soggy. The water they were cooked in was probably more nutritious by the time they were of a texture that Mugwomp could stomach. She would also eat mashed potato but that doesn't really count because everyone likes mashed potato. I think scientific studies were undertaken that proved if you didn't like potatoes cooked this way you were ten times more likely to be a Nigel No Friends. You can't argue with science.

Frustratingly, even as a teenager on the verge of womanhood, Mugwomp is still as fussy as when she was a toddler. If she goes to Subway her order is always the same. Foot-long chicken fillet sub on a white roll, add cheese, lettuce and mayonnaise. I think she may have gotten daring and recently added red onion into the mix. That's it though. What's even worse is, the only topping this kid will eat on a pizza is cheese. Why even fucking bother. Slap some cheddar on a piece of bread and put it under the grill, it's the same thing. She's going to be such a joy to take on dinner dates, I'm sure. As Mr. T would say, 'I pity the fool.'

Finally, we come to my youngest, Boris. While not as fussy as his older sister, he was (and still is) the slowest eater I have ever had the displeasure of knowing. The rest of the family could have finished an hour earlier and Boris would still be sitting there, not even halfway through his meal. The only person I know who eats as slow as my boy is his grandfather, Longshanks. He has an excuse though. The man is so tall it takes an age for food to travel from his mouth to his stomach so he needs to take it easy or he'll suffer serious indigestion.

It's so frustrating watching Boris eat that I have to suppress the urge to either mash his face into his food, or blend it up (the food, not his face) and pour it down a funnel while he swallows it or chokes. It will be his call in the end.

As far as cutlery goes this kid is a lost cause as well. He is one year off of completing primary school and still holds a knife and fork like a one handed, two fingered leper. I suspect I could train a disabled rat how to use silverware correctly before the boy masters this most basic of life skills.

There are times I feel that I have failed him as a parent but then I realise it's not me, it's Karen.

Black Metal Nursery Rhymes

This section will be short and sweet because I'm not bitching about something that pisses me off. Not much anyway.

As a connoisseur of all things heavy metal and horror I have found traditional nursery rhymes somewhat lacking in blast beats and death metal growls. I refused to force feed my children these insipid, vanilla-flavoured songs when I could give them tasty, rocky-road coated brimstone. At first, I would just growl out the vocals of the old boomer favourites like "Mary had a Little Lamb" and "Twinkle, Twinkle, Little Star". This was okay but it felt like I had just taken the easy route and sold out by doing covers. Additionally, these interpretations of the old songs were not conducive to putting my young to sleep. The high-octane vocals just made them bounce on their bed like they were in a one person mosh pit. Something hardcore yet soothing had to be discovered.

I started Mongolian throat singing to the tune of "Song of the Volga Boatmen", also known as the "Yo Ho Heave Ho" song. For amazing examples of this type of singing, check out the band, The Hu. The deep baritone rumble worked a treat and the kids fell asleep as easily as if I had drugged them with morphine.

It was a natural progression for me to create my own nursery rhymes. Here are the two that I still remember. Feel free to use them for yourself, I hold no copyright on them. The first is called "Murder in the Air" and goes like this:

"And there was murder in the air, murder everywhere,
Was Muggy having so much fun, killing everyone,
With her axe and her gun, axe and her gun,
And it was fuuuun."

Yes, those are the only lyrics to this song, but honestly, that's all this instant classic requires. I have used Mugwomp's name because she was the one that I wrote it for, not as any sign of favouritism. I have no preference for any of my offspring.

The tune for this is an old song, circa 1950. I only know it as "Na Na Na Nananananana Nanananana". I tried to find it on the Google but to no avail. Honestly though, use whatever tune you want.

Arming yourself and your little one with plastic weapons and dueling while singing this happy tune makes for some memorable family moments.

My second song is called "Spiders! Spiders! Everywhere!" I don't know the era the tune came from but it goes like this:

"Na Na, Na Na, Na Na Na,
Na Na, Na Na, Na Na Na,
Na Na, Na Na, Na Na Na,
Na Na, Na Na, Na Na Na."

I tried searching the internets for this one as well but yet again it was fruitless. So much for it being the font of all human knowledge. It's pretty simple though. Each "Na" is a different syllable. The fact that you are reading this shows you have a modicum of intelligence so you'll work it out.

Anyway, here are the lyrics:

"Spiders! Spiders! Everywhere!
Spiders! Spiders! In your hair!
Spiders! Spiders! Eat your nose!
Spiders! Spiders! Eat your toes!"

For best effect sing this song while tickling the ever living shit out of your little bundle of joy. They love it.

I guess all I'm saying is don't be limited by the watered-down generic crap they have fed us for generations. Forge your own path and make the songs you sing and the tales you tell a piece of your own family history. It doesn't have to be as twisted as mine but I guarantee that you won't have as much fun if you just take the "normal" route.

Movie Classifications Are Just a Guide Anyway

That's how I feel about them at any rate. My home is my

castle and as Lord, I will be the one to decide what is or isn't appropriate for my family to watch, not some faceless censor that doesn't have the slightest idea of what gets us off.

Karen has a different outlook. Not that she's a prude but she has definitely questioned some of the choices I have made, when it comes to the films I let my kids watch. In my defence, at least they weren't *The Lion King*. Fuck I hate that flick with a vengeance. Both the original and the remake. And the damn stage show. I haven't even seen the remake or the live show but I still fucking hate them. I hate them more than I hate Donald Trump and I despise him more than Screech. For this I lay the blame squarely with Helga. We will explore where this hostility originates shortly.

Regardless of what the missus would argue, it wasn't as if I had actively let my kids watch certain films. It was more like I would be watching something on the TV and they would come in and sit down with the intention of starting yet another pointless conversation. I wasn't going to stop the flow of the movie or show I was watching so they just had to deal with whatever was on the television screen while they babbled, or leave the room. After all, if I had to sit through endless reruns of *Teletubbies* or *Peppa Pig* then they could watch *The Hills Have Eyes* or *Dawn of the Dead*.

When it comes down to it, I can't help that my kids are drawn to the same twisted things that I am and would become engrossed by whatever I was watching. They cannot fight their genetic makeup any more than a termite can stop eating wood.

However there have been some cinematic experiences that I have chosen for Mugwomp and Boris for which I have been held to account. Whether justly or otherwise is not a matter for you to decide either. I have already been judged, so any opinions you may have, are no concern of mine.

When Boris was eight years of age the two of us sat down to watch an animated movie that had just come out on Netflix. The movie was called "Sausage Party". In summary, it is about a sausage and his friends that get bought from the supermarket. Initially they think that they have been chosen to go to food Nirvana but they quickly realise that their actual fate is to be consumed. They spend the rest of the movie trying to get back home. It's all pretty harmless fun with some adult oriented humour but nothing all that shocking. Until the end. The movie finale is a no holds barred food orgy. Even I was taken aback, but considering that the main character was voiced by comedian Seth Rogan I shouldn't have been surprised. As soon as I realised what was happening, I tried to cover Boris' eyes and ears but had limited success. It turns out he didn't know what was being portrayed anyway so no harm was done.

Unfortunately, as luck would have it, that was when Karen came home from work. She walked through the front door and was greeted with her husband and son watching animated sausages, hot dog buns and all sorts of other foodstuffs fucking the shit out of each other in high-definition glory. I gritted my teeth in preparation for the tongue-lashing I was about to receive.

My wife picked her jaw up off the floor and gave me what for.

'M'Lord, what the actual fuck!' she said, pointing to the screen where a hot dog bun was getting spit roasted by a pair of Frankfurts.

Sausage party indeed.

'Oh, babe,' I stammered. It had only been a week since Karen had last chastised me and the wounds were still raw. I was not in the mood for another round just yet. 'You've come in at the worst time possible. The rest of the movie's been tame. Fucking honest. How the hell was I to know there was going to be a food orgy. Please don't hurt me.'

Remember when Karen hurled me around the room like a rag doll after I told her I was going to film Boris being born? Well, that's what I was facing again. I was shitting myself. I looked to my boy and pleaded, 'C'mon, mate, tell your Mum it hasn't all been like this.'

'It's true, Mum. M'Lord didn't know this was going to happen.' he said, pointing to the screen. 'He tried covering my eyes when the food started fighting.'

I glanced at the screen and saw that a donut was currently getting reamed by an ice cream cone. It wasn't a good look so I turned the television off. There was no need for Boris to see food fornicating any more. I don't think there was any need for me to see it either for that matter.

I think this saved me from Karen's wrath. Well, that and the fact that our son was the apple of his mother's eye and had her wrapped around his little finger. If he said that I was innocent then that was good enough for her. I could breathe easy once again.

Another incident that comes to mind involves Mugwomp, our neighbour's daughter and a movie called "This is the End". Yet again, this was a film starring that jester, Seth Rogan. He seems to be a common theme when it comes to movies you should not let young children watch.

Muggy was ten years old at the time and we had asked our neighbour's daughter, Jewel, to look after her while Karen and I went out for dinner. I had taken Mugwomp to Blockbuster so she could hire a couple of DVDs to keep her amused while we were gone. Unfortunately, we had been beaten by the traditional Saturday night stampede and there were not many titles left to choose from.

Yes, I'm fucking old. If you don't know what Blockbuster or DVDs are ask your parents, I have no desire to enlighten you.

I grabbed a copy of *This is the End* from the shelf and read the blurb on the back. It seemed harmless enough, a comedy about the end of the world. I saw that it starred Seth Rogan, James Franco and Jonah Hill and thought with comedians of that caliber that it had to be funny. Mugwomp had already watched *Pineapple Express*, an earlier work by Rogan and Franco, and she thought that was hilarious so I couldn't see the harm. I showed her the cover and she gave it her approval. There wasn't anything else worth hiring so off we went.

Before continuing let me make it very clear that I had not seen this movie at this point in time so I did not know what I was getting my daughter into, let alone the horror I had unintentionally subjected our innocent babysitter to. Sorry Jewel, wherever you are.

Hours passed and Karen and I finally returned home from our night of freedom. We went inside and found Jewel sitting in the living room watching television. Her expression showed something was not as it should be.

'Hey, Jewel.' I said, 'Muggy in bed?'

'Hey, M'Lord. Yeah.' she replied with a troubled look on her brow.

Karen handed her some money for services rendered and probed, 'So, how did the night go? Any issues?'

My wife had obviously noticed Jewel's expression as well.

The young teenager's eyes darted between Karen and myself before she nervously grabbed the DVD cover from the coffee table and handed it to my wife.

'Muggy told me that M'Lord said it was okay if she watched this. Is that right?' Jewel asked.

Karen held the cover up to me, noting the MA15+ rating in the corner before turning it over to read what the film was about. I watched her for a second or two to see if there was anything in her expression that warned of my impending doom. Nothing for now, praise Satan. I returned my attention back to our out of sorts babysitter.

'Yeah, that's right. Why, was there a problem?' I responded.

The wife placed the video cover back on the table and made her way over to stand by me. This was classic Karen. She comes to stand near me any time I may have messed up so she could lash out like a fucking epileptic scorpion.

This is what I live with. I should probably escape while I still can, but much like the relationship between my mother, Maleficent, and my stepfather, Napoleon, the she-devil has my soul and I am ensnared by her beautiful darkness.

Luckily, I saw this move a mile off and I tactically repositioned, so that Jewel was between myself and my succubus. As evil as she was, Karen was still averse to causing harm to the innocent. She saw what I had done and discreetly nodded her appreciation of my maneouver.

Jewel was having trouble giving voice to her concerns which in turn raised my own unease.

'C'mon, darl', speak up,' I prodded, 'Look if it's cos there was drug use that's okay. Not great but Muggy's seen it in movies before.'

'There was that, M'Lord, but there was something else so much worse.'

'Oh fuck, really?' I thought to myself as I felt a knot form in the pit of my stomach.

'Really? Do explain.' Karen purred while mutilating me with her eyes.

'I need to sit down.' I muttered as I flopped into a seat, resigned to my fate. The two girls also took a seat on the lounge next to my recliner.

Before our young neighbour could continue, my daughter ran into the room and jumped into my lap, having been woken by all the talking.

'Hello, Mum.' she called excitedly before turning her attention to me. 'Guess what, M'Lord?'

'What Muggy?'

'That movie was so good!'

'Was it? That's great. What was the best bit?' I asked, hoping Jewel was worried about nothing.

Mugwomp had a bit of a think before she replied, 'The demons were the best. They were the funniest.'

That's my girl.

I looked over at Jewel and saw she was squirming uncomfortably. I was dreading what was coming.

'Were they darling?' Karen interjected, 'Why were they so funny?'

Remember, I had not seen this movie at this stage so what came next was as much a shock for me as it was for Karen.

'Oh my God, Mum, they were hilarious. They had these massive willies and at the end one of them had his cut off. There was blood everywhere. And another one put his in Jonah's bum and possessed him. It was soooo funny.'

'Oh, really?' Karen said.

'Oh no. I'm so fucked.' I moaned.

'I'm gonna go home now.' Jewel called out as she bolted for the door and the sanctuary of her own house.

I can't blame her. I would have run away too if I had that option. With an overwhelming sense of dread, I took Mugwomp back to her room and tucked her into bed.

'Goodnight, Muggy, I love you.'

'Goodnight, M'Lord, I love you too. See you in the morning.' she said as she rolled over.

'I hope so.' I muttered under my breath as I walked back down the hall to whatever fate had in store for me.

'Fuck it,' I thought as I entered the loungeroom, 'The best defence is a good offence.'

If only we had a crucifix in the house but alas, my allegiance to the Lord of Flies precluded such overt Christian symbolism.

There was Karen, hovering a foot off the stained timber floor, arms outstretched. A pair of flaming horns like those of a stag had erupted from her forehead in my brief absence.

'Now, hang on,' I began, 'Before you lose your shit why don't we watch the movie first. Then you can decide if you need to hurt me again.'

She thought on it briefly before agreeing to my terms. 'That seems fair, babe.' Karen said as she ceased her levitating antics and returned to terra firma. Her horns blinked out of existence and she was back to the woman that I had married in what felt like an eternity ago.

Sometimes, the link a pregnant woman has to the netherworld is never fully severed and in times of anger she manifests the demon that possesses her. As you can see, Karen was one of these souls and like every other female in her position, she revelled in the raw power that it gave her.

'So, did you have a good night, M'Lord?' Karen asked, changing the subject. She stalked up to me like a cat on heat, a glint in her eye.

'To a point. You?'

'I had a great night. Does Mr Chuckles wanna play? Could be his last time.'

For reasons unknown to myself, Karen was always in the mood for sexy times after manifesting the beast within.

'Why not?' I said, never one to turn down an opportunity, 'But can you make the horns come back?'

'Sure, who am I to deny a last request.'

Suffice to say I fucked like my life depended on it.

To make a long story short, we got up the next day, watched the offending film and, to be honest, as far as I was concerned, I didn't see what the problem was. I think Jewel had made a mountain out of a molehill.

I looked at Karen sitting next to me and said, 'That wasn't that bad, hey? No big deal.'

She returned my gaze, 'I just don't know, M'Lord. I guess Muggy's seen worse.'

And that was the end of it. My fears were for naught.

I'm of the opinion that whatever entity shares my wife's form enjoyed watching the apocalypse so much that it couldn't bring itself to let Karen cause me harm. She had also been sated the previous night and was in no mood for violence. Thanks again, Mr. Chuckles, I love you.

"Oh God No! Can't We Watch Something Else for a Change?"

Between the ages of about one and four, kids take control of the television. One day you are watching whatever takes your fancy and the next the TV is permanently on ABC Kids or whatever other poxy shit they have on DVD.

This isn't the worst of it though. Like all kids, my spawn had access to so many different viewing options but they would become obsessed with a certain show or movie and watch it, over and over, day in, day out, for weeks on end. Shows I thought were clever when I first saw them became despised instruments of torture.

Honestly, unless it's porn, I cannot watch the same shit constantly without developing some level of animosity towards it.

The worst culprit by a country mile was Helga with her love for the dreaded "Lion King". For close to three years, every time she came to stay with us my eldest would bring a copy of this Disney "classic" to watch. It was bad enough we had to have this film playing constantly but my daughter would also crawl around like a freaking lion cub. I don't know if she was meant to be Simba or Nala and honestly, I don't really care. Fuck all of them as far as I'm concerned.

I'm fully aware that the rage I feel for this movie, it's sequels, the remake and anything else associated with the franchise is totally irrational and I should probably seek professional help but I don't care. I live to hate.

For the sake of posterity, this is how my version of the "Lion King" would go.

Scar kills Mufasa as per the original but instead of letting that annoying shit, Simba, escape, he eats the little fucker immediately and assumes his rightful place at the head of the pride. Then, for shits and giggles, he hunts down Pumbaa and

Timon and makes the meerkat watch while his warthog lover is slowly devoured in front of his very eyes, before he in turn is fed to Scar's dimwit hyena allies. In a show of force, these are then torn limb from limb by the other lions.

Word spreads like wildfire across the African savannah and all that dwell thereon bend the knee to Scar, Tyrant of Pride Rock.

The End.

And no singing. Musicals suck harder than a Dyson vacuum cleaner.

Tales of Sickness and Woe

Children falling ill is a fact of life that I could do without. It's not the whining, they do that on a daily basis anyway and their lethargy is a godsend because you get a break from constantly tidying up the devastation they leave in their wake. It's the vomit. Cleaning up your own oral expulsions is one thing but having to deal with someone else's spew is a whole other level of disgusting. They never seem to make it to the toilet or sink either, which just adds to the repulsiveness of the task at hand.

I can't remember which of my little animals it was but I remember letting one of them sleep in bed with me on a night Karen was working the graveyard shift. It was well past midnight when I felt my youngster sit up suddenly. Being a light sleeper it didn't take much for me to stir. When you read what happened next you will understand why I considered my insomnia a blessing in this case.

'What's wrong?' I mumbled in my semi-conscious state.

'My tummy doesn't feel good.' came the reply.

And then the gagging started from somewhere above my

face. I was instantly wide awake and barrel-rolled out of the bed like a commando under heavy fire. Not a moment too soon. In the dark I heard a choking noise followed by a sudden blast of hot liquid and semi-digested food as it slammed into my pillow. I don't know what I would have done if my head was still in the target area but I'm pretty sure it wouldn't have been conducive to good parenting. Like a man possessed I rushed over to the light switch and flicked it on to reveal a scene of utter carnage.

Sitting in a pool of its own filth my poor child was crying while snot and the remainder of its oral discharge dripped down his or her pyjamas. Where my head had been only seconds earlier was what could only be called ground zero. A steaming pile of God knows what covered my pillow and bedhead. It reminded me of the acid blood that exploded from wounded xenomorphs in the sci-fi classic "Aliens".

'It's okay. I'm gonna run you a bath, just don't move.' I told my distressed offspring.

Like the Colonial Marines from the aforementioned movie I would have rather nuked the site from orbit but unfortunately that wasn't an option.

With the bath running I stripped my tiny spew machine, taking great care not to get any of the vomit on myself. As I carried my kid at arm's length to the bathroom I called out for my faithful mutt.

'Rommel, come here, boy.'

Right on cue he ran up to us, had a sniff of the air and his hairless sibling and wagged his tail, knowing what was coming. I placed the young Chook in the bath, turned off the tap and looked back for my dog. He was gone but the sounds coming from my bedroom told me he was doing what I wanted from him anyway. The general was having a late night snack. As disgusting as it sounds (and believe me, I gag even now when I think about) it was better than dealing with it myself. Dogs can be invaluable in this regard. They will eat most of the mess purged from the bowels of your human-wannabes with relish. Further evidence canines bring more to the table than our own kin.

While Rommel fed, I washed whichever kid it was, making sure to get the chunks from its hair. Then I dressed it and put it into its own bed. Lastly, I grabbed a bucket and gave my Chucky express instructions to use it if they felt like being sick again. Then, taking a deep breath of fresh air, I went back to the mess. As expected, the worst of it had been cleaned up by my dog so all I needed to do was put the bedding in the wash and torch my pillows. There was no saving them.

My apologies for that stomach churning story but the reality is that raising a family is brutal and disgusting much of the time. If you have kids, you already know this and if you don't, hopefully you stay that way.

I promise the next tale is more belly laugh and less stomach churn.

This was definitely Boris, bless his gentle soul. He was three or four, and it was the weekend. Karen was out with her coven and I was home with the boy and Mugwomp. I have a feeling that Rommel had passed away because if he was still alive when this happened then I probably wouldn't have a story to tell.

At this stage it is important that you get a general idea of the layout of our house at the time. It had three bedrooms, one bathroom and one toilet. The most pertinent fact was that the children's rooms were at one end of the house while the toilet and bathroom were at the other. The young fella had been feeling a bit under the weather and was just chilling in his room. I was with Mugwomp in the living room, probably watching "Paranormal Activity" or something.

I went to the kitchen, which was in the general vicinity of the kids' bedrooms, to fetch a snack. Being a caring father I stuck my head in on Boris to see how he was feeling. He was as pale as a ghost and looked like shit really.

'Hey, buddy, how you going?'

'Bad.'

'Did you want to try and eat or something?'

'Smiley fritz and plastic cheese please.'

'No worries, mate.'

I plated up his order and took it in to him, 'Here you go, señor.'

He grinned weakly and took a bite of the processed meat. Bad idea.

Within seconds of swallowing, Boris' complexion went from whitish grey to pale green. It didn't take a genius to know what was about to happen.

'Quick!' I cried, 'Run to the toilet!'

It was too late. To his credit the boy ran like he was being chased by the Devil himself. Out his room and down the hallway he bolted, trailing a never ending stream of vomit behind him. He made it to the throne, flipped up the lid and got the last of it out. A commendable effort but the damage had been done. From Boris' bedroom to the toilet there was a trail of his stomach contents.

A feast for Bear Grylls perhaps, but a nightmare for me.

Mugwomp stuck her head into the hallway, saw what had happened and decided it was a good time to go outside and bounce on the trampoline.

'Thanks for the help, babe.' I called after her as I surveyed my surroundings in disgust.

'You're welcome. He's not my kid.' my girl replied as she shut the door behind her.

See, laziness incarnate. While her father was trying to determine the best way of cleaning up the contents of his son's bowels, Mugwomp had decided to abandon him in his hour of need. If she was there what happened next may have been averted.

I stripped Boris and dumped him in the shower. After he was clean I gave him a change of clothes and plonked him on the lounge with a bucket. Now I had to work out how the hell I was going to approach this disaster. The trail crossed multiple terrain types: carpet, timber, tiles and rugs. This was going to rival masturbating with a cheese grater levels of enjoyment.

But then I had a lightbulb moment, an epiphany if you will. At least I thought so at the time. I grabbed the vacuum cleaner from the laundry and attached the powered head. I was ready to tackle this task like a pro. I kicked on the power and started to suck the filth up off the floor. That was the plan anyway.

It was a bad plan.

Being overwhelmed by what I was confronted with had clouded my judgement. I may have even panicked. Seriously, there was spew everywhere. I truly believe that the part of my brain that housed rational thought went to bounce on the trampoline with Mugwomp that day.

In my mind's eye, I had expected the vacuum cleaner to suck up the solids and most of the slop, leaving me with a fairly simple mop up. The reality of the situation was very different.

The powered head was pulverising the soft, partially digested lumps of food into a paste. It was like putting a corpse into a wood chipper. Rather than stopping, like a true village idiot I persisted in trying to suck up my son's mess until the brushes in the head were so clogged with human waste they were rendered useless. This was still only a minor setback as far as I was concerned.

Casting the head aside I continued to vacuum using just the hose. I sucked a little bit up but pretty soon the moisture in the dust-bag leaked into the electrical components and the thing started smoking. The useless piece of shit was dead. After throwing the deceased vacuum cleaner out the front door like it was a God-botherer on a Sunday morning, I grabbed a linen cupboard's worth of towels and proceeded to sop the gunk up off the hard floors. When it came to the carpet and rug I soaked up what I could and organised a steam clean for the next day.

I told you it was a bad fucking plan.

Dog - 1: Vacuum Cleaner - 0.

Zero stars. Do not recommend.

This House is not a Democracy

In theory, Australia is a democratic society where freedom in all its forms is a given right. I would argue that some people have greater freedoms than others but that analysis does not fall within the scope of this work. For the sake of this discussion we will assume that yes, our country is a working democracy.

My house is not. Within these walls the family unit operates under a benevolent dictatorship led by Karen and myself. Next are the dogs and finally, on the lowest rung are our children.

Mugwomp is currently pushing eighteen and has these funny ideas regarding equality and her position in the family pecking order. After yet another argument concerning her lack of contribution to the maintenance of the property, I informed her that she was welcome to move out if she thought that she was hard-done by.

'You know we aren't forcing you to live here right? If you don't like it you can leave. I'll even hold the door open for you.'

'I can't afford it, M'Lord.' my little demon-spawn pouted angrily.

'So you best do your chores then, huh.'

'Why?' she said indignantly, 'I have a say.'

'Sorry, I don't think so. Why do you have a say?' I asked her as I crossed my arms.

'Whaaaaaat!' Mugwomp snapped, 'Why do I have a saaaaay!? Because I have riiiiights!'

It didn't take much to make this one angry. I didn't care, my daughter was about to learn some home truths.

'You don't get a say any more than you have rights.' I countered, 'Mum and I rule here and what we say goes. There's no discussion. It'll always be that way, darl'.'

'Who do you think you are! The King? WELL, YOU'RE NOT!' Mugwomp raged.

Her mood was starting to rub me up the wrong way. I was getting pissed off.

'AS FAR AS YOU'RE CONCERNED, YES, I AM THE FUCKING KING! AND THE LORD OF MY DOMAIN! AND WHAT I SAY IS FUCKING LAW!'

While it generally takes a lot to rile me up, when I get

going it's like a volcano erupting, and Mount Chook had just blown its stack. To her credit, Mugwomp stood her ground, as she always does. She's either brave or stupid, the jury is still out on that.

'NO, YOU'RE NOT! WE'RE EQUAL!!'

'HAHAHAHAHAHAHAHAHA!' I heard Karen start laughing from outside, where she was returning from hanging out the washing. 'Equal? Muggy, we're not equal.' she continued as she came inside.

I love it when my wife backs me up. It makes me equal parts surprised and aroused.

'AAAAARRRRRRGH!' my daughter screamed through tears of rage, 'YES WE ARRRRRRRE!'

When Mugwomp and I argue we feed off each other's hostile energy. This leads to voices being raised louder and louder in an ever-increasing effort to out-angry the other party.

'NO, WE'RE FUCKING NOT! YOU'RE TRIPPING BALLS! YOU CAN STICK YOUR RIGHTS UP YOUR ARSE!' I roared.

My daughter howled like a witch burning at the stake and bolted for her room. This was good as it let us both step back from the brink of the abyss. Karen went to follow her but I grabbed her hand.

'What are you doing?' I asked her.

'I'm going to go talk to Muggy.'

'No, you're not. She is gonna get a dose of reality my love. I've had enough of her crap.'

'Okay, okay. Calm down first though, babe. I'll just go and talk her down all right.'

Karen was right, I needed to chill out before round two started. I went out to my smoking room, packed a bong, smoked it and packed another before knocking that one back as well. Then I lit a cigarette to calm my farm while my daughter hopefully did the same. Ten or so minutes later the weed had kicked in and I was mellowing out nicely. Never underestimate marijuana's ability to soothe an angry soul. Two cones and I had gone from Idi Amin to Shaggy Rogers in a matter of minutes. I went back inside and joined my wife in Mugwomp's room, where they were sitting beside each other on the bed.

My daughter looked at me with red rimmed eyes. 'So you really don't think we're equal?'

'Of course we're not equal. Before you lose your shit again, answer me this. Who pays for your phone?'

'You and Mum.'

'Who pays for your food?'

'You guys.'

'And all the bills, electricity etcetera, who covers those?' I continued.

'Again, you do.'

'And are you paying rent?'

Muggy saw that she was fighting a losing battle. 'No.' she mumbled.

'Exactly, babe. Your Mum and I make sure you guys want for nothing. So, until you are paying us board, or you know what it's like to pay bills we won't be anywhere near equal. How can we be while we still support your ass?'

She looked to her mother, 'Really?' she pleaded.

Karen patted Muggy on the leg before getting up from her bed and joining me in another rare moment of solidarity.

'M'Lord's right, darlin'. As long as we are supporting you, we aren't equal. We bust our balls making sure you kids are looked after and have a good life. Do you appreciate it?

Fuck no! Stop being a princess and start pulling your weight, my dear.'

Then she gave me a high-five. Winner, winner, chicken fucking dinner. As reality hit my daughter in the face like a shovel she buried her head into her pillow, sobbing like a Collingwood supporter after yet another Grand Final loss. Karen and I left her to process her new reality.

Never give your children the impression that they are on the same level as you. You created them, wiped their asses when they were useless bags of meat and bone, and have made sure that they have been fed, clothed and educated for their entire, pitiful existences. Your spawn should treat you with the respect that you deserve. This should not change just because they are near adulthood in the eyes of the law. They're no more adults than I am Lucifer. Until they know what it's like to eat two-minute noodles five days in a row just to pay the rent, they have no right to presume they are your equals. Useless shits, fuck 'em all.

Rule with an iron fist or your young will run roughshod over you. Don't be an arsehole, unless that's how you roll, but do not let them mistake any kindness you show for weakness. You are in charge and don't fucking forget it.

"Oh my God, really?"

What follows are condensed descriptions of random shit that has occurred over the years. While I have enough material to fill a Bible a few times over, for the sake of brevity, the events I have chosen to include below need only be summarised in dot points. Any attempt at more in depth story telling would be mere waffle.

- In junior primary school Mugwomp was so ashamed that I was an accountant she would tell her friends I made processed cheese for a living. I can't say I blame her.

• On a similar note, Boris used to think that I was a hired assassin. He came to this conclusion after watching the film, "The Accountant", in which Ben Affleck plays an autistic hitman that uses the accounting profession as a cover. I did all that I could to encourage this belief for as long as possible.

• Mugwomp recently admitted that her and her friend Squinty used to defecate in a bush that grew out the front of our house for shits and giggles. Disgusting as it is I still had a good laugh when she told me. This girl just does not give a fuck.

• Five-year-old Boris wanted lightning bolts shaved into the side of his head. I thought I would give it a shot. Poor choice on my behalf. I did not have the skills to cut lightning bolts into his hair. However, I did have the skills to shave his head completely. Karen was beside herself with grief because she thought he looked like a tiny cancer victim. I couldn't stop laughing. He looked like a little thug. It was gold. The icing though was he had his first ever school photos with a head as bald as his backside. That was a good day.

• Mugwomp once tried to cook pasta but failed miserably. I believe she is the only person to ever burn spaghetti black. How did she manage this you ask? Well obviously, she added the dry pasta to a saucepan, and then placed it on a burner. Without any water, as you do. She's a special girl, this one.

• I think that the best punishment I have ever inflicted upon one of my kids was when I took the door off of Mugwomp's bedroom. She had been busted smoking in her room one time too many so had to pay the price. Besides, if I can't smoke inside, I'll be fucked if anyone else can. The tears she wept as she watched me slowly unscrew her door from the

frame, were so numerous, I could taste the salt on the air.
- For a few years now I have been calling Karen and the kids random names. There is method to this madness. If I ever develop dementia then my family will be none the wiser and I won't be shipped off to end my days in a home. I swear if they ever did that, I would haunt the fuck out of them.
- When my children were younger, I used to threaten them with "The Bad Kid Store." We used to drive past a massive, yellow warehouse on a regular basis and I would tell my young that it was a processing facility where parents could take naughty children and exchange them for reprogrammed good ones. Whatever works, my friends.
- Once, when he was about six, Boris thought it would be fun to put the plug in the bathroom sink, turn on the tap and just walk away. Obviously, it overflowed and flooded the vanity unit underneath. While taking everything out so I could wipe the inside of the cupboard dry, I realised for the first time how much shit a woman can horde. No word of a lie, I spent fourteen hours emptying and then refilling that cabinet. The amount of beauty product I pulled out should not have fit in the space provided. It was like the Tardis.
- When I am deep into my cups, I have been known to visit the lavatory and go to sleep. On two occasions someone from the fam has needed to go to the toilet but they have been unable to rouse me. In desperation they have had to rush over to our neighbour's house and beg to use their loo. Lucky for them someone had been home both times or it could have been messy. I guess Mugwomp could have let them use her bush.
- A few years ago, I was in desperate need of some alone time so I hid myself by lying down on the floor on the far side of my bed, invisible from the bedroom door. No sooner had I closed my eyes than I was asleep. Four hours later I awoke to

my family calling out for me and wondering where I was. I decided to stay quiet for another half hour before revealing myself. Be smart and grab moments like this with both hands as they don't come around very often.

Conclusion

Finally, we come to the end of another chapter. I apologise for its length. There was quite a bit of ground to cover but to be honest it was hardly a slog. A trove of valuable information was provided, such as:

1) Feeding young children is the equivalent of flinging shit at a wall and seeing what sticks. Not fun for either party.

2) Homemade nursery rhymes and stories are superior to the tosh that all the vanilla parents sing. Compose your own songs, it doesn't have to be Mozart, trust me.

3) Do not let your little ones watch anything that stars Seth Rogan. It's just easier that way.

4) Kids will spew. It's not if but when, where, what and how much. Be prepared and get a puppy.

5) Finally, and most importantly, make sure that YOU are in charge of your family. You and your partner, if there is one, need to assert dominance from an early age and retain it until your little bastards have moved on to greater things. Be a ruler and not a doormat.

There you have it. May these tales of my homelife serve as a warning to the childless that life is so much better without kids. If it is too late for that then I hope you can take some form of comfort from my misery. Know that you are not alone my brothers and sisters.

Chapter 10:
Family Fun Times, More Trouble Than They're Worth?

I am of the opinion that going out with your spawn, whilst not enjoyable, is necessary to stave off insanity and the violence that comes with it. As much as you would love to, you can't keep your family locked up in the house until they are ready to be cast out into the world. Bad things will happen. Ask that psychotic son of a bitch Josef Fritzl how it turned out for him.

In theory, excursions and holidays are meant to be times when families rekindle the bonds between them. However, in practice, there is every possibility that these trips will tear your brood apart in a flood of blood, sweat, tears and snot. In my experience, this issue compounds the more children you have in your family unit. One child is bearable, but as soon as you add even one more to the group be prepared for things to go downhill. Be aware, the speed of your descent into Hell also increases exponentially the more offspring you add to the mix.

As discussed elsewhere in this manual, the older a child gets, the harder things generally become. This does not hold true with regards to family trips, as going anywhere with your crew is hard work, regardless of their age. When they are babies, it sucks due to the amount of crap you have to take with you, and as your kids get older it still eats a bag of dicks due to the stinking attitudes exhibited by the ungrateful little shits themselves.

Having kids changes the whole dynamic of going anywhere. Pre parasitic infestation you could just go and do things. You could wake up, look to your significant other and say, 'Hey, wanna go and do <insert relevant fun activity here>?'

They would have a quick think and either show interest or not. They may even suggest an alternative adventure if they weren't enamoured by your initial proposal.

As soon as they come on the scene, younglings throw a spanner into the works of an otherwise uncomplicated decision-making process. Rather than doing whatever takes your fancy, suddenly there are a number of considerations you have to take into account:

Is it child friendly?
Are there changing rooms?
Is there alcohol?
Will we be staying the night?
Are we going to be walking much?
Will the kids enjoy it?
Why the fuck bother, what's on the television?
The list goes on. And on. And on.

In essence though, it all comes down to one basic, overriding factor.

What will cause me the least possible grief?

Personal enjoyment does not factor into the equation. You do whatever it takes to make your bottom feeders content so they're not in your face demanding the impossible.

Adventures With Babies: We're Gonna Need a Bigger Boat

That's obviously a bastardised quote from "Jaws" but in

all seriousness if you are expecting your first child, make sure that your car is up to the task. Before too long you will need to transport a shitload of baby related product. Probably more baggage than when you first moved out of home. I'm not even joking.

For example, a simple trip to the shops with your little terrorist requires you to bring the following items:

1) Nappy bag containing: two or three nappies, a packet of wipes, plastic bags to put soiled nappies in, a change of clothes, a bib, snacks, bottle of formula (unless you are breastfeeding), a toy or two, a small blanket for changing nappies, a bottle of vodka (preferably poured into a water bottle), arse moisturiser and a dummy if your kid is that way inclined. There are probably things I have missed but you get the idea.

2) A pram or other baby transportation device.

Remember, you have also forked out a few hundred dollars on a car seat because supposedly it's illegal to put your baby in the trunk nowadays. Yet more proof the government is taking away our freedoms, one stupid law at a time.

This is just for a trip down to the shops. If you were going on a family outing you would need to add a bouncer, leash, even more food and formula, an eski, a heating device to warm your little one's food because God help them if they have to eat or drink their meal cold, a water bottle, a freaking huge umbrella, and even more toys, including a little trike for them to ride around on.

When Karen and I would visit friends with the intention of staying the night we would also have to add a portacot on top of everything else listed.

It's a lot of shit, hey? Shit that needs to be packed into

your car on top of everything else you and your partner normally take with you. As I said, you need to make sure that your motor vehicle has enough storage capacity or you're screwed.

How has it come to this? It's fucking ridiculous. Our ancestors managed with practically nothing, so why do we need so much crap to look after babies and toddlers? It's not like you can just give it all up and go back to how it was in Neolithic times either. Some nosey prick will call social services on you. All because you would rather your kid slept on a reed mat with animals, as opposed to sleeping in a corporatised, piece of shit bed. Bastards like this should mind their own business.

By the way, I will find out who you are and there will be a reckoning, even after all these years. Mark my words. Snitches get stitches, you pizda.

On the bright side, you only have to deal with this logistical nightmare for a year or two, three on the outside. By this time your kid should be toilet trained so you won't need to carry nappies around. If it's not, you need to look at yourself in the mirror and ask if you are really up to the task. It should be walking, so you won't need a pram any more and finally it should be able to sleep on a bed or lounge without falling off so you no longer need to take a cot with you. At last, you can go out without having to bring half your house. A time to celebrate wouldn't you think?

No chance. As your child ages and finally starts developing skills mastered by most other species in weeks, they also begin to develop attitude problems which turn them into rather unlikeable sods. The fact that they are yours also means that you can't just walk away and leave them raging at the base of the escalator.

Unfortunately, they become even more repellent the older they get, but you still have to socialise them. This means, against your better judgement, going out with creatures you would rather have nothing to do with.

Effectively you are exchanging a load of physical baggage for an even greater mental burden. None of the parenting guides tell you this though, do they? Lying bastards!

Out and About With the Gang

Allow me to regale you with tales both humorous and horrific, stories that show what it's really like going out with my family. Be advised, while rarely fun, there are little rays of sunshine through the otherwise perpetual gloom so it's definitely not all bad. I sincerely hope that the next few pages help you to answer the question posed by this chapter's title.

Are family fun times more trouble than they're worth? Read on and decide for yourself.

1) Oh Mugwomp, wherefore art thou?

This story takes place when Mugwomp was only four or five. I know this as Karen was heavy with my third burden, the boy child, Boris. My wife, two daughters and myself were visiting some friends at their new home. The male of the relationship had inherited a substantial fortune from his father and they had used a portion of it to purchase a very old residence in a well-to-do suburb in the Radelaide Hills. This place, while not quite mansion status, was large nonetheless. Suffice to say, it was fully sick.

We had whiled away the warm afternoon eating succulent barbecued meats and tasty cheeses while drinking ice cold ales that dripped with condensation and love. The girls had gone to play with our friends' children in the labyrinth of rooms and corridors, so us adults had been left to our own devices. A rare treat indeed.

As the sun began to disappear over the horizon, Karen and I decided that it was time to make a move. I stuck my head into the back door and shouted, 'Helga, Mugwomp, it's time to go. Get your shit together.'

A moment passed and Helga appeared with our friends' children. A minute more and there was still no sign of Muggy. I called out again, 'Muggy! Stop messing about! We're going so get your arse here now!'

Still nothing so I organised the kids into a search party and sent them back into the house. They returned ten minutes later, my younger daughter still noticeably absent.

'Sorry, M'Lord, we couldn't find her. Dunno where she is.' Helga stated.

So began an intensive search that went on for the better part of an hour. Initially it was a calm affair, but after scouring the house room by room multiple times and still not locating my wayward child, things took a frantic turn for the worse. Karen was starting to panic and even I had become concerned with the welfare of my youngest daughter. We decided to check the surrounding streets in case Mugwomp had gone for a stroll. After fifteen or so minutes of running about the neighbourhood calling her name everyone met back at the house, empty handed. Karen was in tears and was about to call the police to report her missing.

'Let me just do one more sweep of the house first, babe.' I told her while hugging her about the shoulders.

Mugwomp and I are very alike in many ways. Even at her

young age I could not rule out some tomfoolery on her behalf because that's the way I would roll. I went back through the house and analysed it with the eyes of a demonic four-year-old. Eventually I came to one of the kid's bedrooms. As is common with all children, the room was a bomb site.

I scanned every detail like the T-1000 searching for John Connor. At first, I didn't notice anything and with a knot forming in the pit of my stomach, I was about to return to my distraught wife, still minus a child.

That was when I saw a strange lump under a blanket strewn over the top bunk.

'Did that move?' I thought, 'Yeah, that moved.'

I stalked over to the bunks and flung the blanket into the air. There, curled up into a ball and giggling like a paralytic leprechaun was my daughter.

'Oh, you little fucker!' I said, also starting to laugh. 'We have been looking everywhere for you!'

Mugwomp's response, 'I know.' Then more laughter.

I scooped her up and made my way back to Karen.

'Your Mum is going to go ballistic. I hope it was worth it.'

'Yep.'

We returned to a scene straight from the pages of Shakespeare. You could taste the drama in the air. Karen was unceremoniously sprawled across a divan, back of her hand pressed to her brow, while the rest of the group hovered about like sympathetic mourners. This only increased our mirth and try as we might, we couldn't stop the renewed fits of laughter. All eyes immediately turned in our direction.

'Hey! Look who I found.'

'Muggy!' Karen leapt to her feet and bounded over to me.

A miraculous feat considering her significant girth. If we were outside, she would have caused a solar eclipse.

She snatched her daughter from my grasp. 'Where were you? I was so scared! Don't ever do that again!'

Karen was doing that thing relieved mothers do where they simultaneously scold and kiss the child that caused them to fear for its life. Personally, I was torn between relief that we found her unharmed and pride in Mugwomp's twisted sense of humour and determination to see a gag through to the end, consequences be damned.

I have never been more concerned for any of my children's safety than I was that day. Well done Muggy, well fucking done.

2) Boris and fishing go together like boiling oil and cold water.

For Boris' seventh birthday he was given a fishing rod and the associated tacklebox. It was fair to say he was stoked and keen to give angling a crack. I had my doubts as to how much he would actually enjoy the realities of going fishing though, considering his temperament.

Boris was, and still is, a boy that struggles with sitting still and doing nothing. He has to be active, physically or mentally, every waking minute. He doesn't shut up either. I've heard him conduct complete conversations in his sleep, clear as day; not the mumbled gibberish more common with talking in one's sleep. And he doesn't give a shit if you are interested in what he has to say either, he'll keep going regardless. Boris has had me cornered and mercilessly pummelled me with facts and figures relating to his beloved soccer, knowing full well I couldn't give a rat's arse. It is maddening.

The fact that being a successful fisherman involves a great deal of sitting still in silence means I knew this was going to be a terrible idea. Nevertheless, I hooked up a day with the Hermit, a keen angler, for the three of us to go throw in a line and try our luck.

The day came for our expedition and we loaded up the car, bought some bait and off we went. After driving for about an hour we found a promising spot. We could see good sized fish swimming about and the weather was fair. It had all the potential to be a good day. I couldn't have been more wrong.

Within five minutes of setting up his rod Boris had cast and reeled in his line probably a thousand times, scaring off the school of fish we had seen. On his last cast he got frustrated and smashed his rod against a tree, obliterating it completely. Due to all the fish scattering to the four winds the Hermit suggested we try a different spot so we drove to another location and the two of us cast in our lines while Boris explored the area. Predictably, it didn't take long before the familiar moans started.

'I'm bored, can we go now?'

'Not yet mate, me and Uncle Hermit are gonna fish for a little while. Why don't you tell us some facts about Cristiano Messi.'

'It's Cristiano Ronaldo, M'Lord.' he corrected.

'Whatever, impress us with your knowledge.'

Boris bombarded us with pointless information for around a quarter of an hour before he realised that neither of us were listening.

'M'Lord, I wanna go home. Fishing sucks.'

With a huff, the Hermit reeled in his line and began packing up.

'Fuck it,' he muttered, 'Let's go. The fish aren't biting anyway.'

I could tell he was at wits end. Fishing with a whining seven-year-old wasn't his idea of fun and Boris had tested the limits of his patience. We packed up in silence and drove home listening to the boy drone on about God knows what.

As I had expected, that was a complete waste of time. Over two hours of driving for a grand total of thirty minutes fishing. The Hermit hasn't asked us to go fishing with him since and that was over five years ago.

If only I could escape my family so easily.

3) That's not how you do Father's Day.

Fourth of September, 2016. A date that goes down in infamy in the annals of Chook family history as the worst Father's Day ever.

In my opinion, the ideal Father's Day involves a pub lunch followed by a relaxing drink in the comfort of my own home. Preferably alone.

That's why the Royal Adelaide Show happens at the same time. So mothers can take their children to the show while dads get to chill the fuck out in peace and quiet.

This was not the case in 2016.

Mugwomp had started high school that year at an agricultural college where she had joined the Alpaca Club. One of the requirements of this society was to present the animals at The Show in a competition against other alpaca breeders. As luck would have it, this competition took place on the fourth of September, Father's Day. My day.

It started much like every other preceding celebration of the sperm donor. I was woken way too early with the customary greeting.

'Happy Father's Day, M'Lord.' came the chorus as Boris and Mugwomp flung themselves onto the bed between Karen and myself.

I opened one eye and peered outside. The sky was only just beginning to lighten. This was much earlier than the norm.

'In the name of the Cloven-Hoofed Lord, what are you guys doing? It's not even light outside.' I groaned.

'Muggy's got to show her alpaca remember?' Karen mumbled from the other side of the bed.

'Grrrrrr, that's right. What time do you have to be there, daughter of mine?' I asked as the rest of my vital systems slowly came online.

'I've got to meet the rest of the group at nine o'clock.'

'Really? What time is it now?'

'Six thirty.' my wife answered.

I groaned and rolled onto my back while my family presented me with gifts. They mustn't have been anything to write home about because I don't remember what I was given. Mind you, the rage I was feeling by day's end was so intense it could well have erased any other memories of Father's Day from my mind.

'Did you want some bacon and eggs?' Karen asked me.

'No thanks. It's too early to eat.'

I tried to close my eyes and get a little bit more sleep while my clan stuffed their faces but to no avail, so I rose from my bed, showered and got dressed.

Mugwomp's competition started at ten a.m. By my calculations it couldn't go for more than an hour so I would be home by midday and could spend the rest of the day doing absolutely nothing. Karen could not begrudge me that, as I would have fulfilled my parental obligations by supporting my daughter in her endeavours. The day would still be a good one.

We were at the showgrounds by nine sharp and our girl took off to meet her group while Boris, Karen and myself wandered about aimlessly for a little while before making our way over to the arena where the alpacas would be put through their paces. Karen located a program which showed the order in which the animals and their handlers would be presented. As my daughter's school started with a "U", they would be the last of approximately a dozen competitors.

This was the precise moment my anger began stirring, like a hot ember slowly being brought back to life.

I nudged Karen, who had started gasbagging with another child's mother.

'Hey, how long do you think this will go for?' I asked her.

'I don't know, M'Lord, an hour, hour and a half.'

Try four. Four hours we stood there while a multitude of kids I did not give a fuck about paraded their animals back and forth in front of a largely apathetic crowd that applauded unenthusiastically. By this stage, I was livid. It was after two p.m. I should have been home hours ago. I glanced at Boris and he looked as enthralled as I was.

'How much longer, Dad? I'm bored.' he moaned.

I was so angry that his use of the "D" word did not merit my immediate attention.

'I dunno, mate. This sucks balls, hey?'

He nodded with more gusto than he had shown all day, poor bugger.

Only Karen still retained her enthusiasm for the event, curse her soul.

'Oh, look! Here she comes!' she called out, taking photos

like an obsessed paparazzi.

We watched as Mugwomp led her alpaca around the arena for a grand total of two minutes.

I've always considered alpacas a second-rate animal, a poor man's llama if you will. This experience had not changed that opinion in the slightest.

Two minutes. We stood around for half the day so I could watch my daughter lead her stinking beast around for two freaking minutes.

'That's it?' Boris exclaimed incredulously.

'You have got to be kidding me!' I began, 'We hung around for that? What a fucking joke!'

I noticed a handful of other parents nod their heads in agreement.

Karen opened her mouth to speak, no doubt in an attempt to put a positive spin on what had just transpired. I was having none of it and shut her down before she could get a word in.

'No, you don't. That was shit.' I said as I placed two fingers over my wife's lips, 'There is nothing you can say that will make me think otherwise. Look,' I pointed at Boris, 'We've been here so long the boy's grown six inches.'

Before the wife could respond Mugwomp appeared beside her.

'Well, that was crap.' she said.

'Not wrong there, love.' I replied, 'Let's go home.'

'Actually, I'm gonna hang out with my friends. I'll be home later, is that okay?' Muggy asked.

'No worries.' I looked at Karen and the boy, 'Let's go.' I said as my second-born disappeared into the crowd of people that had grown steadily since the morning.

Boris and his mother both gave me a look that told me this

shit-full day was far from over.

'C'mon, M'Lord,' my soon to be ex-wife stated as she embraced me around the waist, 'We're here now. Let's go get something to eat, have a couple of rides and look around for a little while.'

I was seething with fury and extricated myself from her clutches, 'You have got to be kidding me, right?'

I was about to unload but noticed that the young fella was on the verge of tears. He had been subject to the same shitshow as myself and it had taken its toll on him as well. Some cheering up was called for.

'Okay, let's hang around for another couple of hours. We've been here this long, we may as well go and have a bit of fun, hey?' I was still majorly pissed off, but the boy deserved to do something enjoyable after the hell he had just endured.

'Thanks, Dad!' he said as he ran over and gave me a hug, headbutting my skull shaped belt buckle in the process.

'No worries, mate, but listen, you ever use the "D" word when you talk to me again and I'm taking you straight to The Bad Kids Store, all right?'

'Yes M'Lord, sorry, M'Lord.' Boris apologised as he rubbed the red welt on his forehead.

I tousled his blond locks playfully, 'That's my boy.'

Karen sidled up and took my hand, 'Thanks, babe, Happy Father's Day.'

'Yeah, Happy fucking Father's Day indeed.' I quietly muttered as we fought our way through the crowd to the food court.

Don't get me wrong, as a child I loved The Show. Sideshow alley, rides, show-bags, it all kicked ass. Even as a teen it was cool to go to. Getting stoned on the chairlift before going on the Super Loop was an annual tradition. Then, at seventeen, I moved out of home for the first time and I came to realise the true value of money. Going to the show became an indulgence that I could not afford. A few years passed and I was probably in my early twenties before I finally went to The Show again.

I fucking hated it. I hated having to pay some bullshit entry fee for the privilege of spending even more money once inside. How greedy is that! You either pay to get in and the rides are free or its free entry and you pay for the rides. Anything else is just double dipping.

The highway robbery didn't end there either. Everything on the inside cost two to three times more than what it was worth. The tight-ass in me had an aneurysm every time I paid some thieving, inbred carnie my hard-earned cash for a ride on his rusted, clapped-out death machine.

Last, but definitely not least, I hated the crowds. Why is it that wherever I go, I'm the only one that knows their destination? Everyone else wanders about like lobotomized council workers. Just work out where you're going and stay the fuck out of my way. Please.

I postulate that I only truly reached adulthood when I developed a loathing for The Royal Adelaide Show and its ilk.

Once again, I have drifted off like some senile old fool so I must beg your pardon. We shall return to the worst day of my life post-haste.

So the three of us finally managed to force our way through the stinking mass of humanity that flowed like some corpulent river between our party and the sustenance we craved.

'Let's just get something cheap,' I said.

'Hotdog, chips and a drink?' Karen suggested.

Boris and I agreed that was the way to go. Three dogs with sauce, three servings of chips and three drinks later and our bank balance was seventy dollars lighter. My angronometer went up another couple of notches as I paid the money to the web-fingered, genetic freak manning the till.

Look, I don't want to dwell on this shit-full day any longer than I have to. It pisses me off to think about it even now. To cut a long, painful story short we went on a couple of overpriced rides, bought Boris some ridiculously empty show-bags and then spent the next five hours going from stall to stall while Karen sampled the products on offer.

My mood was irredeemable by this stage. There are few things I hate more than what is effectively window shopping. Karen tried to get me to taste random things but I was seething. It was all I could do to not go postal, so I just grunted whenever she spoke to me. She even tried to placate me with a beer but I was so fucking mad that it evaporated into steam the moment I grabbed the glass.

It was nine thirty at night by the time we got out of there. We had lurked for so long, Mugwomp had managed to locate us again and we drove home in silence. The family had never seen me so furious before and I think they were in fear of their lives, even that devil bitch that tricked me into marrying her. I stopped at a bottle shop on the way back and bought a litre of Jack's finest, knowing it was the only thing that could ease my pain.

As soon as I pulled into the driveway, I grabbed the bottle and stormed off to my shed where I drained its contents in record time. Wisely, the family left me to my own devices and

I woke up in the morning cuddling the one I loved the most, my dog.

4) To trick a trickster

Recently Karen, Boris and myself were at a shopping centre looking at getting me a sweet pair of walking shoes. Coincidentally they were an early Father's Day gift but that is where the similarities between this story and the prior one end. In this tale it is I, not my cursed bloodline, that is triumphant for a change.

Karen was in need of the little girl's room, which was located down a fire escape corridor. Boris and I waited at the end of the hallway while she went and did her thing. My heir, who was eleven at the time, noticed a vending machine about a third of the way down the hall and decided a scare prank was in order (as I've said, the apple doesn't fall far from the tree).

He hid himself behind it and whispered to me, 'Let me know when Mum is coming.'

I had a snigger before responding, 'Okay, I'll put my foot on the wall when she comes out the toilet.'

As I was already leaning against it, this was an inconspicuous signal. Boris gave me a thumbs up in response and sat there like Gollum waiting to ambush Frodo.

He was delusional if he thought I was going to go along with his plan. I waited a couple of minutes and a complete stranger walked out of the female restroom.

She made her way towards us.

I looked at Boris for a second to build up tension then slowly lifted my left leg and rested my foot on the wall as the young woman closed on his position. Eagerly, he pounced on who he thought was going to be his mother. Foolish boy.

'Boo!' he started shouting at the same time he realised that the lady in front of him was not his dear, old Mum.

The look on Boris' face was priceless. He had turned a beetroot red, mouth open mid scream as his voice died in his throat. His feet were rooted to the spot with arms raised in the classic scare pose. I exploded into a fit of uncontrollable laughter, tears streaming into my manly beard.

'Oh my God! That was gold! I wish I had filmed it!' I somehow managed to cry out.

As his "victim" continued to her destination she also started to titter. Boris rushed me and flailed his fists against me but it was like a solitary gnat biting on a rhinoceros' arse.

'Boy, I got you so good. You should have seen your face. HAHAHAHAHAHAHAHAHA!'

I was still laughing as Karen rejoined us.

While Boris told her what I had done, my expressions of joy continued unabated.

My eyes streamed, and I could not stop sniggering all the way back to the car.

Finally, I stopped and wiped the tears from my eyes, only to start up again as the scene played through my mind's eye on a continuous loop.

'C'mon, M'Lord, give it a rest. You can stop laughing now.' Karen chastised as she opened her door.

'I can't though!' I wheezed as I struggled to draw breath.

Try as I might, which wasn't very hard, I just couldn't control myself and laughed all the way home.

Boris was livid but my care factor was less than zero. For once, I had won.

Remembering this moment makes me happy. Fuck, it was funny.

Five stars. Thoroughly recommend.

Holiday or Helliday: Our trip to New Zealand

On the twenty-ninth of October, 2011, Australia's major airline decided to ground its entire fleet, both domestic and international. This was a reaction to some of its staff seeking better pay and working conditions. A rational, measured response, I know. Well, along with seventy thousand other people around the globe, this decision had stranded the Chooks. We were trapped in Sydney. Not an ideal situation as far as I was concerned.

Credit to the company though, they paid for us to stay in a swanky upmarket apartment and covered all our costs for the three days we were stuck in old convict town. As an added bonus they gave us free return flights to anywhere in Australia or New Zealand. Obviously, we chose to take a trip over to the land of the long white cloud. The fam had always wanted to visit the home of Hobbits and Jake the Muss and this was the perfect opportunity.

Before continuing, let me make it absolutely clear that I do not have a bad thing to say about New Zealand. I don't think there is a more beautiful land or people anywhere on the earth. Karen and I love the place so much we want to live there.

If it wasn't for the kids, it would have been the trip of a lifetime. No word of a lie, Boris four, and Mugwomp nine, fought constantly. Two days in and Karen and I had taken to having a couple of shots of tequila for breakfast just so we didn't kill them. Nevertheless, despite the little beasts' best efforts, it wasn't all terrible.

For fear of sounding like a tour guide here are some highlights that made this trip unforgettable.

1) Racing a blizzard at Mount Cook.

This was scary fun. We were on the road to somewhere fucking amazing when weather warnings started broadcasting over the radio. A blizzard was bearing down on our location and the road to where we were going had been closed due to extreme weather conditions. In fact, roads were being closed down all over the place. We were in danger of having to ride out the storm in our car. That would have sucked harder than a starving calf.

Karen checked the Googles and the closest place of refuge was near Mount Cook, back the way we had come from. Undaunted, I ripped on the hand brake and flung the car through one hundred and eighty degrees before flooring it, dark, doom-laden clouds broiling behind us. I drove like the great Ricky Bobby and weaved through the winding mountain roads, managing to keep just ahead of the storm. As I slid into our destination the blizzard broke around us, reducing visibility to practically zero. It was awesome.

As we made our way to reception to check in, we managed to lose the kids in the near complete white out engulfing the land. Unfortunately, they found us.

2) Watching the Bledisloe Cup in Kaikoura.

Kaikoura was our first destination in New Zealand, a cool little coastal town on the South Island. It was dinnertime so we decided to check out what was on offer. After cruising up and down the main road through town we decided on a rowdy pub called "The Whaler". It was the night of the first game of the Bledisloe Cup and the bar was packed with locals expecting that their mighty All Blacks were going to dominate the

Wallabies at home, as was so often the case.

We entered the swinging saloon doors and the crowd fell silent, giving us a quick once over. It was obvious they knew instantly that there were Australians in their midst. Karen went up to the bar to ask for a table and the kind waiting staff gave us pride of place, directly beneath the big screen TV that was going to be showing the game. I have to say that subtlety does not seem to be a strong point of Kiwi culture. They were going to have some sport with their new friends from across The Ditch.

I would love to say that our boys in green and gold stomped the New Zealand team into the dirt but sadly, that was not the case. For all of the first half and most of the second the All Black juggernaut smashed through the Aussie team like a bull through a matador's intestines. We weathered the good-natured ribbing from the locals with grace.

And then it happened. Australia broke through the line and scored a try! Our only points for the game. I was not going to let this opportunity pass me by.

I rose from my chair and faced the crowd in front of me, arms raised in the air in triumph.

'Take that, you motherfuckers! Aussie! Aussie! Aussie! Oi! Oi! Oi!' I bellowed at the top of my lungs as my family tried to hide under the table.

Instead of pounding me into a red smear as the wife and kids expected, everyone in the packed bar applauded me with as much enthusiasm as I was showing.

That's when I fell in love with this country and its people.

3) Queenstown.

If I ever move to New Zealand this is where I would live.

There is just so much to do here. If Karen and I had come to this country child free, the people of Queenstown would be singing of our debauchery for generations to come. Alas, we had to reign in our excesses because it was a family holiday. How dull. I could go on for pages about everything we did here but I won't. Go see it for yourselves. To whet your appetite, here is a taste of what we experienced.

- I ate the best pizza I have ever tasted. Wild boar and venison with a plum sauce. Every other pizza is bread and grilled cheese in comparison. By the way, the name of the pizzeria was Hell's Pizza. This town was made for me.
- Mugwomp, (remember she was nine years of age), schooled adults twice, even three times her age when she completed the Canyon Swing. This involved jumping from a platform, into a ravine, before swinging out to your doom with a bungee rope attached to your ankles. And she did it twice. She made me look like a little bitch, that's for sure.
- Getting tattooed with Karen and then going to party with the tattoo artist at his house afterwards. I learnt that New Zealand is actually made up of just the South Island. The North Island is an aberration that isn't a part of the country.
- We went skiing one day and put Boris into day care. He was so impressed that he spent the day crushing every snowman built by his fellow inmates. He had to assert his dominance somehow, I guess.
- The Fear Factory. This place was a haunted house on meth. Electric shocks, gropey deviants, it had it all. Here was where I regained my manhood after being emasculated by my daughter on the Canyon Swing. The kids couldn't even get through the first room without losing their shit. Luckily the staff let them wait in the foyer with them while I forced Karen

through the house of horrors with me. To her credit, she made it all the way, which I did not think she would be able to do.

Queenstown was a blast, it's a must-see destination if you ever visit our friends across the Tasman.

4) You can get grog anywhere.

This may be a common thing in other countries but in my home state of South Australia, bless her backward soul, the only place you can buy alcohol is in a bottle shop or a pub. In New Zealand you can buy grog from the supermarket. What's more, you can just take your empty containers and refill them yourself. How fucking sweet is that? When Karen and I discovered this, we thought we were in heaven. All the more due to our increased dependency on tequila to keep our children safe. This cemented our desire to move to this country.

5) Lake Tekapo.

Not only are the hot springs to die for, the water in the lake is pristine. I had no issue drinking straight from the lake itself whereas if I did that back in Australia I would probably die. It wasn't just here either, everywhere we went the water was clear. I don't know what angel tears taste like, but I'm pretty sure it's close to what I drank from that waterhole.

6) My one criticism.

While our trip to New Zealand was one of the best holidays the Chooks have ever been on, I would be lying if I said I wasn't slightly disappointed. One thing I wanted to do was hunt Hobbits and, unfortunately, this activity was not on offer anywhere.

If Karen and I ever moved there I would look at setting up a paintball park where paying customers would have the opportunity to go on Hobbit safaris. Not only would I provide gainful employment for midgets and other vertically challenged adults, I would be meeting a previously unsatisfied demand in the tourism market.

I am not the only one that wants to shoot little people with hairy feet, I guarantee you.

Conclusion

So, are family fun times more trouble than they're worth? Like most aspects of child rearing, there is no definitive answer. I think it depends on the circumstances. If it looks like your children are going to be trouble that day then leaving the house probably isn't worth the effort. While this is often the case, remember, like a dog, if you don't provide them with stimulus, they will start to destroy or devour everything. At some point they will need to be taken out. All I can suggest is to take a hip flask or a premix two litre bottle of bourbon and Coke with you on your journeys. It will take the edge off.

However, if your offspring are constantly out and out little bastards then yes, you are probably better off not ever inflicting them on the public at large. Develop a drinking and/or drug problem and have those years when children are part of your life drift past in a perpetual haze.

Alternatively, have a look at yourself. If your kids are out of control, it is more than likely your fault. Harden up and do your fucking job.

Just sayin'.

Chapter 11:
School and Sports, Where Did It All Go Wrong?

So much has changed since I was a burden on my parents. Nowhere is this more apparent than in the education system and children's sports programs.

When I was a kid, your teacher was called "Mr.", "Mrs." or "Miss", not Tim or Jane. What is with this first name bullshit that's all the rage at school these days? Teachers aren't your children's friends, they are your surrogates five days a week. I know I don't let my kids call me by my first name. Christ, I don't let my wife use my first name for that matter. Teachers should be shown the same respect and be called by their titles, not the names their partners call out in the throes of passion.

My teachers were not averse to dealing out the odd caning either. I remember my first day of grade three where our art teacher introduced the class to "Willy Sting", a metre ruler he used to punish unruly students. Today, an educator would be reprimanded just for calling a child stupid, even if it was true. How are they supposed to retain order in the classroom if they can't use fear as a tool in their disciplinary arsenal? The mind boggles.

What's worse, nowadays parents are expected to take an active role in their child's education. Why? I've done my time and have no desire to revisit those days of old. It wouldn't be so bad except the way that they are taught to do things is blatantly incorrect. Maths, for example, why did maths change? I don't have any idea how they do sums now. You can't show your kids the correct way of doing it either, "Because that's not how we do it at school". Like I give a shit. The way they do it at school is wrong.

While on the topic of schooling, I do not see the need to have all these parent/teacher interviews in grades one through to seven. I honestly don't care what my kids' teachers have planned for the year. It is primary school after all so I'm not expecting anything particularly earth-shattering. I have better things to do with my time. Inserting bamboo splints under my fingernails comes to mind.

On the subject of torture, don't get me started on school concerts and the like. As parents we need to take a stand against these mind destroying evenings. Young children are talentless hacks. Having to watch your own kid perform their latest stunt, a tumble roll, for argument's sake, is tedious enough. When you have to waste an entire night watching a whole class of these little losers stage some avant-garde performance dreamed up by their attention starved teacher, you really have to ask yourself if being a good parent is worth the return on investment.

Children's sports have become soft as well. In my day we had winners and losers and losing a game of football, while unpleasant, did not scar a child for the rest of his days. We rewarded talent as well. Today, they don't even keep score until kids are older. What the fuck is that all about? Children need to know what it's like to win and more importantly what it feels like to lose. It builds character and prepares them for adulthood, where they are going to experience many failures and disappointments before they meet their hopefully non-violent demise.

I will end this rant shortly but there is something I need to get off my chest. I'm not a fan of participation awards. How have we become so enamoured with celebrating mediocrity? It is a phenomenon that has only reared its head in the past twenty or so years. The ancients didn't recite poems about Syphilius the Mild-Mannered Scribe. They immortalised heroes like Hercules, son of Zeus and raised their drinking horns to legends such as Beowulf, slayer of the monster Grendl. Even in modern times, at least until the turn of the century, we lauded those that were a cut above the rest of humanity.

Today we make a big deal over our little ones just giving things a shot. Sure, as parents we need to encourage them to try new things, but we shouldn't celebrate it to the detriment of rewarding those children that show true talent. I was shit at sport when I was a kid, but I still played Aussie Rules and cricket. I never expected to win any awards though. Playing was reason enough for me. The highest accolade I ever received was "Most Improved" in primary school football and I was stoked with that. I never begrudged those that received "Best and Fairest", they had earned the recognition. If anything, they gave us lesser mortals something to aspire to.

Ironically, we are setting the current generation of children up for failure by not teaching them how to fail.

The thing that scares me about this is that these kids will be the adults that are running the show when I'm old and shitting my pants. Competent leadership doesn't come to mind when I think of how things will be handled. In all honesty though, the more I consider it, the more I realise that they can't be any worse than the current batch of movers and shakers we have in charge of our futures. Maybe my worries are for naught.

Enough of this, the ravings of a madman at best. Here are some anecdotes, listed under the name of the relevant child, for your reading pleasure.

Helga

Due to circumstances out of my control there isn't much I can say about my firstborn's schooling. Her Mother did what she wanted, with no input from myself. As a result, I was denied the pleasures of attending parent teacher interviews and their like. My disappointment is surely tangible.

We were lucky enough to have Helga come live with us during her final year of high school. However, there isn't much I can say about it. Seventeen-year-olds don't really communicate with their elders and contact with the school was thankfully negligible. One thing I did find strange though was that they held a graduation ceremony and dance before the students had sat their final exams. How the hell did they know if they had even passed? This is the ultimate participation award in my eyes. It cheapens the whole experience for those that actually put in the hard yards when they have to rub shoulders with the likes of myself, who royally screwed up their final year.

It's literally putting the cart before the horse.

When she was younger Helga took up karate for a while. I may not have mentioned it but my eldest is also my shortest child. At four foot, ten inches fully grown, to say that she is vertically challenged is an understatement. She was even shorter when she was enrolled in her self-defence classes.

If I ever get my Hobbit Safari up and running, she's going to be my Bilbo Baggins, mark my words, but before this idea was even a spark in my demented mind, I had other plans for my daughter. The combination of diminutive stature and martial arts training had me convinced she would be a wonderful cat burglar. I was all set on becoming a real-life Fagin, sending my little ninja out into the dead of night to relieve the rich of their burdensome wealth. I ran my idea past Karen.

'Karen, my love, I've just had a brilliant idea.'

'Okay, and what may that be, M'Lord?' The scepticism oozed from my wife like puss from an overripe pimple.

'You know how Screech has enrolled Helga into karate classes?'

'Yeah.'

'I might teach her to become a cat burglar.'

'I think that's the dumbest idea you have ever had.'

That was the end of that. Once again, I wondered why I married this woman. To this very day, her lack of vision is a constant thorn in my side.

Mugwomp

My second-born proved herself to be a handful even before she started school proper. Like so many, Karen and I were slaves to the machine and necessity demanded that we place our daughter into childcare. Initially we enrolled her in one of the large, commercial centres but after they raised their fees, we decided we would give family day care a shot.

Karen found a nice lady that lived around the corner from us who looked after about a half-dozen other little rug rats. Mugwomp liked her well enough so we signed her up. It was great to start with, but it didn't take long for relations to sour between our daughter and her carer.

Mugwomp has a problem with authority. A trait I find endearing, unless it is my authority she is fighting against. Like me, she doesn't like following rules and the woman tasked with her care had plenty of them. Naturally my daughter started to rebel.

The result was that our child of Satan snapped the mind of this poor lady. This is no exaggeration. I came home from my place of indentured servitude to find Karen sitting in my shed, crying, while Mugwomp was in the lounge room watching "Giggle and Hoot" or some other inane garbage, oblivious to her mother's distress.

I greeted my little girl before joining my distraught wife, steeling myself for what was coming.

'Hey, what's wrong, babe?' I enquired as I sat across the table from Karen.

She blew her nose, wiped her tears away and said, 'Muggy's been kicked out of family daycare.'

I launched into peals of laughter, which Karen thought was totally inappropriate for some reason.

'SHUT UP!! IT'S NOT FUNNY!!'

I managed to rein in my amusement enough to respond, 'What do you mean? Yes, it is, it's fucking gold. Our daughter has been expelled and she's not even four. What did she do?'

'Do you really need to ask, M'Lord? You know her as well as I do. The little bitch doesn't listen. She just does whatever she wants. Her carer couldn't hack it any more. When I picked her up this arvo she refunded next fortnight's fees and told me not to bring my little devil back.

'I begged her for another chance, but she told me Hell

would freeze over before Muggy was welcome back in her home. Babe, our daughter fucking broke her.'

And then the tears started to flow once more.

I couldn't bring myself to be angry with my youngest daughter. I found the whole situation hilarious, but to prevent Karen's mood degenerating into something dangerous to my person, I kept my mirth internalised.

'She'll be right, darlin'. We'll just send her back to the other place. At least we got our money back. I'm gonna go have a chat with Muggy.'

I gave my wife's hand a reassuring squeeze before joining my daughter inside. Sitting on the lounge next to her I turned off the TV and sat my second-born on my lap.

'So, how was childcare?' I asked.

'Bad.'

'I heard. Mummy said you broke the lady there.'

'Yep.'

'Do you know you can't go back there again?'

Mugwomp gave me a shit eating grin, 'Yep. Good.'

I chuckled, shook my head and gave her a kiss on the forehead before putting her back on the couch, returning to Karen, who had calmed down now.

'Sounds like the woman was just soft, my love.' I stated.

'Yeah, I guess. Muggy liked the other place better anyway. More kids to play with.'

'There you go. Problem solved.'

A few months later Karen heard on the grapevine that this lady ended up having a mental breakdown. Moral of the story: do not fuck with Mugwomp.

When she hit school, things were no different. Muggy was a hellraiser. Luckily for her though, her personality was infectious, and all the teachers loved my daughter regardless of her disdain for rules.

A highlight from her junior primary school years was when she was caught with a group of older boys and girls sitting on the play equipment swearing like hookers in the Cross on a Friday night. The school informed us that our girl was the creator and ringleader of a school swear club where the kids would sit around swapping profanities they had learnt from their parents. Fucking trippers.

Even Karen saw the funny side of this.

High school was the same. Well, there wasn't a swear club, but Mugwomp continued to make an impression on anyone who had contact with her.

My favourite story from her secondary school years was a tale of subterfuge worthy of being immortalised in prose.

We used to hang out with this mad couple that had emigrated to Radelaide from the north of England, before they moved on to sunnier climes. Mugwomp was in love with their accent and had learnt to mimic it very accurately. She put her impression to the test in her very first year of high school.

One day she had a relief teacher who spoke with the same accent as our friends so she thought she would have some fun at his expense while testing the accuracy of her impression. After a conversation that I obviously was not privy to, my girl had convinced this poor bloke that her family had moved from Yorkshire to Australia the year before.

When Muggy told Karen and me, we were in stitches. It was the funniest thing we had heard for a long time. What made it even better was that this guy was from the same part of England that Mugwomp had professed she had come from.

Impressively, she managed to keep this going for five

years, all through high school, even when this teacher's daughter, who attended the same school, joined my princess' circle of friends. I don't care who you are, you have to admit that is some first-rate bullshit artistry right there. Mad respect deserved and given.

As far as sports go, Mugwomp tried her hand at a few things. In primary school she played netball where, under Karen's expert tutelage her team won the Grand Final. She has played women's Aussie Rules, where she was also part of a successful premiership winning team. I intend on discussing her time as a gymnast.

From a young age, until just after she started year eight, Mugwomp trained three or four times a week for at least four hours a session. That is fucking insane. I don't see why little kids need to have such an intensive training regime. Granted, if they are potential Olympians, train the shit out of them, but the vast majority of these young girls are not even close to being in that category. As Muggy can testify, their bodies are broken by the time they reach twelve or thirteen years of age. If they pulled it back a bit, I'm sure the physical harm done would be greatly reduced. My girl's ankles, hands, back and neck are wrecked, and for what? Not a damn thing. Kids that want to do it will love gymnastics regardless, they don't need to be worked into the ground.

Now that's said let's discuss gym comps. These events can span multiple days, from dawn till dusk. You will only see your kid compete for about ten minutes of that. The rest of the time is spent watching other people's children do their thing. Trust me, the boredom becomes palpable. To make matters worse, the backing track for the competition's floor routine section is blaring constantly from the gym's speakers. The same music.

On repeat. For eight hours a day. And just when you think it's over there is an awards ceremony that will be guaranteed to go for at least another hour. All the while you have to sit on hard wooden benches which have a very real chance of giving you piles.

I think this must be what Heaven is like.

Boris

One year, our family went camping in Mount Gambier for a few days over New Year's Eve. Boris would have just turned seven. Him and Mugwomp had met a few other kids around the campgrounds and as Chooks do, they decided to have a little fun with their new friends.

Between the two of them they came up with the story that Boris was adopted, his real name was Watson and that he was born in Texas, U.S.A. No shit, while these two can cause me a mountain of grief, the stuff they come up with is genius.

Skip forward a couple of months and we were attending the dreaded annual parent/teacher interview. Karen loved them of course. It goes without saying really. First, Boris' teacher (we'll call her Miss Freckle as, unlike the kids, we weren't on a first name basis) discussed the planned curriculum. Same shit, different year. No surprises there. Then she pulled one of our lad's books out and handed it to Karen as I started developing that glazed look you get when you have no interest in what is going on around you.

'Who is Watson?' Miss Freckle enquired.

That brought me out of my reverie.

'What?' Karen and I responded.

She tapped the front of the workbook with her standard issue, blue, Bic ballpoint biro. I remember thinking that she must be new to her career as she had yet to purchase a pen of higher quality. We looked to where she was pointing. Written there, in a barely legible scrawl, was the name, "Watson Chook".

'Who is Watson?' she repeated, 'Your son won't answer to Boris, only Watson.'

Freckle was in teacher mode now and was questioning us like we were the ones responsible for the boy's little mind games. I guess genetically we were.

'No idea.' said Karen.

'Nope, not ringing any bells with me either.'

We obviously knew exactly where Watson came from.

'He also says he was born in Texas.' Miss Freckle continued, signs of stress clearly visible on her face, 'Sorry, but he's doing my fucking head in!'

The struggle was real. I looked at my wife and found she was also near breaking point.

'Don't worry, we'll get to the bottom of this.' Karen mumbled as she took my hand and we walk-ran out of the classroom.

We made it a few steps down the corridor before nearly dying of laughter.

'I can hear you!' came a tearful wail from the classroom we had just escaped from.

'Sorry Miss Freckle!' we cackled as we ran down the hall and back to the car like a pair of escaped lunatics.

We managed to get our shit together by the time we got home and called Boris into the kitchen for a chat.

'Hey, Mum. Hey, M'Lord.' he said as he took a seat on his mother's lap.

'Hey, mate.' we replied in unison. What a team.

Karen took point on this one. 'So, Boris, you know we just saw Miss Freckle, right?'

'Who's that?' he asked, his moon-like face scrunched up in confusion.

I butted in, taken aback by his sudden lack of mental acuity. Boris was the most intelligent of my offspring.

'What do you mean, "Who's that?", it's your teacher. Did you hit your head while we were gone?'

'You mean Sarah?'

Seriously, what is it with young'uns being on a first name basis with their teachers? This practice needs to be crushed out of existence like the dinosaurs.

'Yeah whatever. Do go on, my dear.' I commented in disgust, handing the floor back to my wife.

'Okay,' she continued, 'So we saw Miss Fr, sorry, Sarah, right?'

Boris nodded while eagerly ramming his forefinger up his nose, all the way to the second knuckle. Impressive.

'Well, she asked why you write "Watson" on your books and don't answer to your real name. Wanna tell us why?'

''Cos I like Watson, better than Boris.'

I was not gonna let that slide, 'Hang on a sec, my son, what are you talking about? Boris is a strong name, a name of kings and warriors. Watson is a shit name.'

'Nah.'

'Fuckin' yeah.'

This went on for a little while before Karen silenced both of us with her trademark demonic howl.

'Honey, can you please just use your real name? It's hurting your teacher's brain.' she asked our youngest.

'Okay, Mum, I don't wanna hurt Sarah's brain. I like her.'

'Thanks, buddy.' Karen squeezed her son lovingly, 'You're such a good boy, you know that?'

Boris hugged her back and then went back to his room to continue with whatever he was doing before we interrupted him. Probably trying to end world hunger or something equally virtuous.

When it comes to sport, Boris is naturally gifted. It doesn't matter what it is, if he shows an interest in it, he will excel. This ability must come from his mother's side because, as stated above, my achievements in the sporting realm are lacklustre at best. The alternative is that he is not mine, which in turn can only mean one thing.

That Boris, like Christ himself, was the product of immaculate conception. There could be no other reason. It would also go a long way to explaining why the kid is just so damn nice. He is nothing like the rest of us. A light of redemption in a pool of darkness, that's what he is.

His great love in this world is soccer, or football if you're talking to him. I remember taking him to some "come and try" sessions when he was a wee lad. While all the other kids struggled to even get boot to ball before falling on their arses, Boris was dribbling his ball around the course laid out by the coaches like freaking Maradona. He was a natural.

It wasn't long before we signed him up to a local club. The first season was a disaster. Every game was the same. Both teams would run towards each other from opposite sides of the pitch and slam together in the middle like a mini wall of death. It was more like watching a rugby match than the beautiful game. Even at this young age Boris would get frustrated at his teammates' lack of skill and he would just storm off the pitch in tears. It would be worse if they were losing.

This right here is why it's bullshit that they don't keep score in kids' sports. The officials may not be keeping a tally, but as much as I argue otherwise, the little buggers aren't stupid. They know who's kicked more goals.

Anyway, he stuck it out and now plays in an age group where they keep a tally and all the teams in the competition are playing for the premiership, which is as it should be. The icing on it all is that he has taken out "Best and Fairest" two years in a row, but who's counting.

Boris is now of an age where he runs rings around me, regardless of the sport we are playing. To counter this, I resort to using my size and martial arts skills to get the better of him. This gets him so pissed off. He calls me a cheat, but I would argue that I'm just playing by the rules of the street.

I need to be careful though. He could make the big time and be my meal ticket out of this dreary existence.

Conclusion

I feel I need to apologise. Reading this chapter back, it is more humorous than horrific. That was not my intention at all. It may be that it was because I was recollecting times when my children were in the care of others. These memories are always the happiest, so my mood was probably reflected in my scratchings.

Do not let that lull you into thinking that parenting is not all that bad after all. It is, it is so, so bad. If it wasn't then this book would never have been written.

You end up paying a crap-ton for education and woe betide you if, like Karen and myself, you have multiple kids, because then you can say goodbye to any money being left to spend on yourself. This state of poverty will last for years to come. Fortunately, it is one expense that can be justified. Even though modern teaching methods leave a lot to be desired, for six hours a day, five days a week, your offspring are someone else's problem. You cannot put a price on this.

Children's sports are in a similar position. They also cost a bit of money and are unfortunately a shadow of their former selves. My advice is, if you go into kids' sports thinking that you're paying for your sprog to learn some sporting skills, then you are going about it all wrong. If you look at it as an investment in a few hours of solitude each week while they train, then it becomes a much fairer trade off. Time is money after all.

Yes, you will have to go watch your youngsters play games on the weekend, sometimes at abominably early times, but that's cool. You would be spending that time with them anyway. At least this way they aren't your responsibility until the game ends. Additionally, you get to talk to other adults without being interrupted by your demanding little psychic vampires, which is a rare treat as a parent.

If you're smart like me, you could consider starting a betting pool and turn the season into something quite profitable. Not that I would do that. It is illegal after all.

Lastly, you could be lucky, and the right genetic combination has resulted in a child that has talent in his or her chosen sport. It would be foolish not to nurture this ability on the off chance that they are successful and can carry the rest of the family on their coattails to better things.

Chapter 12:
Pets Are Better Than Kids. Here is the Proof

Deep down, you all know this statement to be true. Tell anyone that has both children and animals sharing their home that they have to choose to evict either a pet or a child. I guarantee you, if they are not soft in the head, that their spawn will be on the street one hundred percent of the time, without fail. Pets are cheaper to look after, they're tidier, they care for your wellbeing, and they're much less demanding than human young. Honestly, they just bring so much more to the table.

If you are still child free and have made it this far, the preceding eleven chapters should have already convinced you to give up on having your own kids in favour of adopting some loyal fur babies.

For those of you who are still undecided, a pox on your soul. It is because of you that I am forced to write this final chapter. It should not have been necessary. Chapter Eleven was meant to have been it, done and dusted.

However, as one of the goals implied, way back in the introduction to Part One, was to convince people that they should cut back on reproducing and spend their days basking in the love of a pet instead, I have to present all the evidence I have at hand. I would be doing you, the reader, and this project a disservice if I started cutting corners now.

To this end, I will conclusively prove once and for all, beyond a shadow of a doubt, that having animals in your life is a far superior option to mating with the intent of propagating the species. This shall be established, as is the case throughout this treatise, through the use of real-world examples experienced first-hand by yours truly, M'Lord Chook, patriarch of the Chook family.

Let us begin.

1) Pets develop at a much faster rate than humans.

I have said it before, human infants (Homo sapiens), are effectively sacks of meat for nearly a year after their V.E.D. Even after they become ambulatory, they do not develop any useful skills for many, many years. Useless doesn't even begin to describe them.

Compare this to these common domesticated animals found in a typical Australian household:

- **Dogs (Canis lupus familiaris):** walking within four weeks of being born and weaned by six weeks of age. They can start to be trained at eight weeks. Police dogs are walking the beat by the time they are eighteen months of age, two years max.
- **Cats (Felis catus):** mobile by three weeks of age and killing native wildlife within a month. A cat will never be trained. Ever. They are little fuckers, one and all.
- **Snakes (Serpentes), Reptiles (Reptilia):** these critters are fully independent as soon as they come into the world. Dumb as two planks so cannot be trained. The emphasis on cannot as opposed to cats' "won't".
- **Birds (Aves):** depending on the species, birds are

ready to fly and actually leave the nest between 2 and 10 weeks after hatching. Some are highly intelligent and can be taught tricks and can even learn to talk in a few months. Other than that, they do not have much utility.

- **Fish (Osteichthyes):** just like our cold-blooded companions listed above, fish are doing their own thing the moment they hatch or are born, depending on how they're feeling at the time. They are incapable of being taught a damn thing.

Every one of these animals is living its best life within weeks of entering the world. While not all are trainable, the same goes for humans. Regardless, the fact that they are independent means you are not constantly looking after them for years to come. Give them a bit of food, fresh water and some occasional stimulation and they are happy as a pig in shit. As I have documented throughout this manual, this is not the case with our own children. Far from it.

A special mention should be made regarding dogs. Yes, they are a lot of work until they are around eighteen months of age because they just do not give a fuck. This can be alleviated through a strict regime of exercise, training and discipline. When it comes down to it though, it is only a year and a half, two on the outside before your dog becomes bearable. Based on my experience, we cannot say the same for our own young.

Being pack animals, they also love spending time with us. This obviously means doing things with them to keep them happy. This is hardly a chore. Unlike kids, dogs love their families unconditionally. They would die for us. Would your own flesh and blood? I didn't think so. A daily walk is a small price to pay for their companionship.

Pets — 1 : Kids — 0

2) Pets bring more joy than kids.

While writing this dirge to parenthood I found it was a struggle at times to come up with examples of when my children gave me joy. On the other hand, the pets Karen and I have shared our lives with were a constant source of amusement. Here are some memories that sprang to mind:

- Rommel, a pittie cross, was the first dog I shared with my wife. He would destroy everything Karen owned, even though we were together when we got him. Shoes, clothes, underwear, car headrests, you name it, he ate it. What an amazing way for my boy to show his undying love for me. The feels were real.
- As he got older, Rommel would love trying to mate with our friends. If that isn't a friendly dog, I don't know what is.
- I remember we adopted the local stray cat for a little while. It eventually outstayed its welcome when it took one swipe too many at another staffy we had called Chopper and he showed it the door. Up until that point in time though the cat was a barrel of laughs. It was hysterical when a young Boris would put it in the garbage bin and close the lid. Or when he would throw it onto a sleeping Chopper. As you can see, Boris and Cat had a special relationship. Like He-man and Skeletor. Those were good times.
- Then there were the times that my snake and tarantula escaped. These were separate occasions, but the results were the same nonetheless. Let's just say that much hilarity ensued. While I searched for the little bugger, whichever it was, Karen

learnt to sing in a higher pitch than she thought possible while practicing her table dancing. Hide and seek with creatures that you love, while being serenaded by your woman, does it get any better?

- Boris had an ant farm once. They were interesting little critters, walking about in their tunnels doing ant things. But then the boy decided to unplug the hoses that joined the farm pieces together and walk away. The little fuckers got into everything. Ant farms were banned that day, but it was through no fault of their own. As with everything that turns to shit, human activity was to blame.

- One last memory worth mentioning was the time I took a baby Bird-Eating Spider called Cuddles on vacation with the rest of the family. Karen refused to travel in the same car as the tiny spiderling but rather than stay home as I insisted, she drove her own car. As per normal, the kids were monsters for the whole holiday. They drove us batshit insane. Not a peep from Cuddles though, she was so well behaved, we didn't even know she was there. I occasionally remind Karen of this fact when she starts to sing the praises of the spawn of our loins.

I have barely scratched the surface when it comes to the joy my animal companions have brought into my world, but it is obvious that a life without pets is a joyless one. On the other hand, a life without children has near limitless potential.

If you still need convincing think on this. The opposite of joy is misery. If you experience less misery in your life, you are obviously happier. No great revelation there. Those of you with both kids and pets in your lives, ask yourself which ones get into trouble more? Which ones do you yell at more? Which ones would you rather abandon?

If you don't answer, "My children." you are lying to yourself.

That being the case, it only stands to reason that because your pets are causing less misery in your lives than your offspring, they are obviously the source of greater joy.

Pets — 2 : Kids — 0

3) The death of a pet causes the most grief.

You don't get to my age without attending a few funerals. I have paid my respects to the young, the old and many ages in between. At some I felt nothing, at others there was a tinge of sadness and at fewer still I shed tears of loss. Even rarer ones brought on happy tears.

Nothing hurt me like the deaths of my dogs Rommel and Chopper. I was cut to the core of my being and the grief is still so strong that I have to fight back tears as I write this. They were my boys, and I don't think I need to go into any more detail as far as those days are concerned. I respect their legacy too much to try and wring any cheap humour from their passing.

On the other hand, the death of a goldfish called Bubbles is fair game.

Mugwomp's first pet of her own was a black, boggle eyed goldfish she obviously named Bubbles. While he meant nothing to anyone else in the family, he was everything to our little girl.

As happens with all fish, one day Bubbles was found floating belly up in his tank. Muggy prodded him with a finger a couple of times.

'Yep, he is dead all right.' our daughter stated matter-of-factly.

The wife and I breathed sighs of relief from her bedroom doorway. We had been expecting her to lose her mind with grief. Karen gave me a pat on the butt before walking over to our eerily calm child.

'Can I bury him in the backyard?'

'Sure.'

'Hey, Muggy,' I suggested, 'Why don't you flush him down the toilet so he goes for one last swim?'

'That's a great idea, M'Lord.' Mugwomp replied calmly, 'Can you please get me the net.'

The fish's death hadn't really registered yet. This was the calm before the storm.

I grabbed the little net from under the laundry sink and brought it to my girl, who took it and promptly scooped the little black body out of the aquarium. Then, in single file, we solemnly made our way to the toilet. After we all said a few words about how awesome Bubbles was, Muggy dropped him into the bowl with a plop. Her hand hovered over the button that would send the fish on his final journey.

'Goodbye, Bubbles. I love you.'

The girl pressed down, and her first pet disappeared in a tide of water and antibacterial cleaning product.

That's when the penny finally dropped.

'BUBBLES! COME BACK BUBBLES!' the poor lass cried out in soul searing pain as he went round the "S" bend, tears flowing like a torrent down her cheeks.

I knelt down beside her, seeking to offer her a shoulder to cry on. 'Sorry, darl', he's gone now. Off to a better place.'

My daughter gave me a shove, pushing me off balance into the hallway.

'Get out!' she wailed before slamming the toilet door shut and locking it behind her.

I had never heard waterworks like that before. It was like the biblical flood had started in my lavatory. Until that point in time, I had always thought the term "wailing and gnashing of teeth" was just a phrase ripped from the scriptures. That day Mugwomp proved it was more than that. We couldn't see it but the whole street could hear it.

Such wailing.

Such gnashing of teeth.

I can't tell you exactly how long she was locked in the toilet for. From memory it was about four days. We had to hire a Port-a-potty.

These two tales prove that a pet passing away causes a greater sense of loss than the death of most people. Only those closest to us can hope to evoke the same levels of grief as the empty feeling you get when an animal leaves your life.

It's like an inverse to the idea presented in *Point 2)* above. The more grief you feel when someone or something you know leaves this world, the more joy they must have brought you while they lived.

If that's the case, it doesn't look good for the hairless apes that are our young.

Pets — 3 : Kids — 0

As expected, a whitewash in favour of our animal family members.

Conclusion

I rest my case.

I am sorry for the morbid tone this book ended on, but I needed to prove, once and for all, that pets are better than kids. If, after all the evidence that has been presented, not just in this chapter, but all of the preceding ones, you still believe that having children is better than the company of an animal companion, then there is nothing more I can do for you. You are, as they say in the old country, lost fucking causes.

You probably believe the Earth is flat as well. Losers.

Epilogue: Thanks for Coming

So, we have finally come to the end. From the lows of childbirth, to the highs of animal companionship, this tome has run the full gamut of human emotion. I know it was a wild ride, but as your conductor, I thank you for joining me on this journey.

It is my hope that I have opened your eyes to the lies that brainwash us into believing that having children is one of the greatest experiences of the human condition. Surely my story shows otherwise. It is probably one of the worst choices you could ever make in your life.

Granted, not all parenting experiences are as dire as mine, but truth be told, most are so much worse.

While it is too late for those of you who already have a brood of your own, take solace in the fact that you are not alone. We are a legion of tortured souls and our pain is eternal.

If you are one of the lucky, childless few, for the love of all you hold dear, stay that way. Our planet doesn't need any more humans on it. Be part of the cure, not the disease.

And if you are still blinkered to the reality of parenthood, go for a walk outside. Look at the faces of all the mothers and fathers encumbered with children. Are they smiling? Do they look like they are living their best lives? No, they fucking don't. If that doesn't tell you anything about the reality of family life, then nothing will. In the words of Forrest Gump, "Stupid is as stupid does."

If I have any regrets in putting these revelations to paper, they would be that there was so much information I failed to impart. Helicopter parenting, assassination attempts, and hunting unicorns were all stories I wanted to tell, but alas, time and word count was always going to be against me. For that, I am deeply sorry.

The Dark Lord willing, I'll be able to escape the accursed clutches of my Addams Family wannabe's long enough to divulge more wisdom.

    Nefariously Yours,
    M'Lord Chook.

    P.S. The mental scarring should only be temporary.